DAVID IN SILENCE

DAVID

N SILENCE

* *Veronica Robinson*

ILLUSTRATED BY *Victor Ambrus*

J. B. Lippincott Company

PHILADELPHIA · NEW YORK · 1966

* A C K N O W L E D G M E N T S

My warm thanks are extended to the following for their help and active encouragement: Miss N. Wilkinson, Headmistress, St. Thomas's School for Deaf Children, Basingstoke; Mr. E. Brown, Headmaster, Heston School for the Deaf, Hounslow; Mr. A. E. Heys, Headmaster, Tewin Water School, Welwyn; and Dr. P. Gorman, Librarian, the Royal National Institute for the Deaf.

✳ CONTENTS

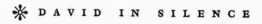 DAVID IN SILENCE

I

* *The newcomer*

The redheaded boy was standing on a chair at the window doing something to the curtain rail, but Michael was too far away to give him a hail. He was about thirteen, and Michael was looking forward to having another boy of his own age to go around with. He watched for a while, until the boy climbed down and withdrew into the darkness of the room behind the open window. He might come out, but the minutes passed and there was no further sign of him.

Michael Guest sat down in the scruffy dry grass on the edge of the Bank. He looked over the roofs of the estate, over the gray murkiness of the town, and across to the hills of Shropshire and Herefordshire far in the distance; but in the hazy and smoky stillness of July they were almost imperceptible.

From this height the harsh sounds of the Black Country town below were softened, though the rhythmic thudding of the steam hammer from the nearest factory drifted up the hillside, booming firmly as always. In the middle distance a good

train struggled up the long slope from the Severn valley. Michael watched the white spouts of steam and heard each blast, but sight and sound did not coincide. The train reached level ground in a flurry of spouts and blasts as it gathered speed.

Michael leaned back on his elbows. School term had ended; it was summer, and he relaxed into the browned grass of the Bank.

A new sound drifted up the hillside: the chimes of the ice-cream van.

Gwang-gwing-gwang-gwong-gwoing-gwoing. He saw the van for a moment as it turned the corner to stop outside Bitter End station.

"Eileen!" He heard his brother's voice raised across the estate. "The ice cream's coming!" And Tommy ran across the grass to fetch their fourteen-year-old sister.

Michael felt the loose coins in his pocket and slowly stood up. As he made his way down to the top row of houses he could hear Paul's petulant voice:

"But I want two ices." Paul was only nine and lived next door but one to the Guests.

"Oh, Mum, but I want two." There was the sound of tears in his voice coming from the open kitchen door; and Michael knew he was deliberately drooping his shoulders and pouting. As Michael climbed over the fence into the back garden, Paul ran down the path at the side of his home with a frolicking kick in mid-air which plainly showed he had won his way.

Michael strolled across the triangular patch of grass which served as a general playground for this end of the estate, and joined a group of boys standing near the swings. Eileen was there, clutching her purse and chatting to some of her friends, while his young eight-year-old brother Tommy looked on.

Gwang-gwing-gwang-gwong-gwoing-gwoing. The white van

with a sugary-pink cone ice painted on either side turned up from the main road and pulled in at the corner. Paul clamored to be served first because he wanted to buy an ice cream, eat it, and then buy an iced lolly. One by one the children claimed their ices and turned away to sit around the swings while they licked and sucked. Two or three older boys hung back before buying iced Cokes in order to show their superiority, and they then teased some of the girls for sucking lollies.

Only Paul stayed by the van, eating his ice and waiting until the last minute before spending his final sixpence. He amused himself by tracing out with a finger the dusty outline of the pink ice cream painted on the side of the van. He did not notice that the other children had dropped their voices and were now speaking in whispers to each other. They were watching the house across the grass, the house which had been empty until last night.

Down the short concrete path the redheaded boy was walk-ing, and they wondered if he were coming to the van and if they would have a chance of finding out what he was like. He was carrying a basket, so he might be going down to the shops; but when he came across the road he strode on to the grass towards them. Satisfied, some of the boys rolled over on their stomachs to watch him more closely.

It had been nearly dark last night when the new family had arrived at number seventy-eight. The father had been there all day unpacking, but the others had come in a taxi long after the furniture-men had left: their mother, a boy of about seven-teen, and this redheaded one.

"He's got freckles," Eileen whispered to her neighbor as he came nearer.

"That won't make any difference to a carrotty temper."

Paul had finished his ice cream and was sucking the pineap-ple lolly.

No one said a word as the redhead boy handed the ice-cream man a list, and there was still silence as he put the bottles of orange, and lemon barley juice, and a large pack of vanilla ice cream into the basket. He took up an ice for himself, put some money on the counter, picked up the change, and finally mumbled his thanks. Then he turned. For a moment the group by the swings stared at him, and he stared back. As someone was about to speak, the boy smiled shyly, and without a word turned and walked back across the grass.

"What's your name?" asked Michael.

"There's no need to go off. Come and talk to us."

"Where do you come from?"

"Don't be in such a hurry."

"Hey, Carrots, come back and tell us your name!"

The boy walked on without turning round. Stealthily Paul ran after him, and when a few paces behind he walked in step with the boy in front.

"Carrots, carrotty, carrotty, carrots," he chanted. "Carrots, carrotty, carrotty, carrots."

The boy looked over his shoulder to see who was following, grinned, and crossed the road into the house. Paul shrugged his shoulders, and while the ice-cream van moved off to the far end of the estate, he came back to enjoy the remainder of his lolly.

"He's mad," was his only comment.

"He's got very bad manners," said Eileen. "It's rude not to answer when you're spoken to."

"Stuck up kid," said someone else.

"We needn't have anything to do with him if he's going to be all la-de-da."

"He looked quite nice," said Michael. "Most redheads are good fun."

But all the same, Michael frowned.

2

* *"You'd better ask him"*

Almost all of those who lived in the Council estate had come from the surrounding district, and it was unusual for people to move to this small Black Country town from farther afield.

Windbell Edge Estate lay between the town of Blackley and the former village of Bitter End. Blackley is one of the many towns that have grown up around Birmingham, and now there is nothing to show where one ends and the next one begins. Roads, canals, factories, row upon row of grubby little houses, railway sidings and sheds, waste land and dumps help to form one of the ugliest parts of England.

Blackley, however, is more fortunate than its neighboring towns, for it lies at the foot of a range of hills. Windbell Edge Estate was built on the foothills, and above the top row of houses were fields that curved upwards and over. It was not possible to see the country beyond from the estate, but the children did not mind, for they had the hill behind and above them; the railway and the canal below.

When the furniture van had arrived outside number

seventy-eight yesterday, the address across its sides proclaimed it to have come from Llandudno. Many of the local people went there for their summer holidays; and it seemed strange that anyone living by the sea and the Welsh hills should come here.

It was much later, after the encounter by the ice-cream van, that Paul disclosed the news. He was sitting with Eileen, Michael, and Tommy, who was about his own age, on the canal bank. They began talking about the boy and his odd behavior that morning, and he said:

"He's deaf and dumb."

"What?" asked Tommy.

"Are you sure?" asked Michael.

"Yes. I heard someone tell my mum. And it means he's mad. He can't talk properly but only makes noises—like a pig," and he sniggered.

"What's deaf and dumb?" asked Tommy, who was slower than Paul and always prepared to take his lead.

"It means he can't hear and can't speak," explained Michael.

"Why?"

"I don't know why. He just can't."

"If he really is deaf and dumb," said Eileen, "that would explain everything. And you shouldn't laugh at him, Paul. He can't help being like that."

They were silent for a while, each of them following their own line of thought, until presently Eileen spoke again:

"You know," she said, "he can't be dumb, because he spoke. He said 'Thank you' to the ice-cream man. Don't you remember?"

"And he can't be deaf either," said Michael, "because when Paul ran after him, he turned round. He must have heard him."

"He turned round," said Paul, "but he didn't say anything. He's mad."

"But he didn't answer us when we spoke to him, so I suppose he didn't hear us," said Michael. "We'll have to try shouting."

They tried shouting at the next opportunity. It was at tea-time that evening, and walking back up the road from the canal they saw the boy a little way ahead, on his own and looking as if he might have been out exploring. Michael and Eileen, Tommy and Paul had a hurried conference in whispers. Paul wanted to call after him as he had done before, but Michael restrained him. Instead they ran on tiptoe to catch him up, and then Michael stopped the others and went on alone.

When he was a few feet behind the boy, he called out: "Hey!"

Nothing happened. He closed the space between them to about three feet, and again—but more loudly—called: "Hey! Carrots, are you deaf?"

The boy continued to stroll up the road, watching the shunting engine in the railway siding as he went. He did not appear to realize there was anyone behind him.

Michael waited for the others to catch him up.

"He's putting it on," said Paul loudly, so that if the boy heard he would know that they were not to be taken in.

"I don't think he is," said Michael. "Let's try again all together."

To Tommy, who followed Paul around wherever he went, this was a great game. Eileen was frankly curious. Though she had heard of deaf and dumb people, she could not believe that this boy was himself deaf and dumb, for he looked so completely normal. In spite of his curious behavior that morning, his smile was attractive, he looked as if he could be good fun, and she still hoped he was taking them in with a cunning practical joke. Michael wanted to get to the bottom of the mystery, so for a third time he went forward, with the others following close behind.

They crept to within a few paces of him. Michael put up his hand as a signal. They took a deep breath, and were about to yell in unison when the boy in front moved to the edge of the pavement, and looked back down the road. He had stepped out to cross the road before he saw them, and then he stopped.

Michael's arm was still poised above his head, and they all had their mouths open. Tommy and Paul had begun to voice their cry, a "Hey!" which died as they watched the boy in front. His expression changed rapidly from surprise to bewilderment, to recognition, and back to bewilderment. Michael dropped his arm, and they tried to look as though they were walking home to tea. The boy waited as they drew nearer. He smiled, and then he spoke:

"'Allo."

It was now the other faces which expressed bewilderment and surprise.

"He can talk," Paul cried.

Recovering himself Michael smiled and walked up to the boy.

"Hallo," he said. "We thought you were deaf and dumb; but, as you can obviously talk, you can't be dumb. What's the great game?"

For reply the boy smiled again and held out his hand. Automatically Michael shook it, though he thought this was rather unnecessary.

"What's your name?" he asked, but the boy had turned away and was now ceremoniously shaking hands with Eileen, Paul, and Tommy, and to each of them he said a polite "'Allo."

Michael gaped, and the others were silenced by the formality.

"Why didn't you speak to us before?" Michael asked when he had recovered himself.

"We yelled at you but you never answered," said Eileen.

"Can you hear us?" Tommy and Paul spoke together.

The boy looked from one to another of them, and with an apologetic smile he pointed a finger at each ear and shook his head.

"De-af," he said. "De-af."

"What?"

"He is deaf. He can't hear us," said Paul almost with a note of triumph.

Eileen's generous and homely nature wanted to comfort the boy for his affliction but, faced with someone who could not hear her speak, she was at a loss how to express herself. She let out only an involuntary "Ah!"

Michael tried to take the situation in hand. He moved close to the boy, leaned over his shoulder, and yelled:

"Can you hear me now?"

A shake of his head was the only reply.

No one knew what to do next. They stood in a row facing him, embarrassed, self-conscious, and trying to realize that here was someone with whom they wanted to make friends, and who lived between their two homes, but to whom they could not speak. They did not mean to appear bad mannered, but they stared at him. It was the boy himself who took the initiative. With a movement of his arm that implied an invitation for them all to join him, he led the way across the road and back towards the estate.

Michael and Eileen walked on either side of him, while Paul and Tommy dropped behind to whisper. It had not yet occurred to them that whether they whispered or shouted made no difference, but it would have seemed wrong not to whisper. Michael and Eileen were feeling the same constraint. Eileen started to say something but stopped. If she leaned forward to speak across the boy, he would see and might wonder what she was saying; and if she dropped behind to talk to Michael, he might think they were being unfriendly. She thought of raising her voice so that Michael could hear her without having to get closer, but that, too, felt wrong.

Only the boy was at ease, and when Michael took an occasional sidelong glance at him, he even looked pleased with himself.

So they walked across the grass in silence, and only once did an odd grunt come from the strange boy. Paul nudged Tommy, but did not dare to giggle while Michael and Eileen were so close. Eileen was thankful that none of the other children of the estate were there to overhear. She felt her own cheeks flushing for the queer noise that the boy made.

They crossed the road, and noticed that their mother had seen them from the sitting-room window.

"Come on," she called. "It's sausages and chips."

"Coming," mumbled Eileen, feeling ill at ease, and wondering if she dared to add that their companion was deaf. He could not hear, so there was no reason why she should not; but for all that she felt it was wrong to speak of his disability while he was present. Paul, however, had no such inhibition.

"He is deaf," he called. "He can't hear a word we say. And he does grunt—just like a pig." But Mrs. Guest had moved away and did not hear.

"Paul Danks, go home at once and mind your manners," Eileen and Michael said, facing him squarely. As Paul scuttled off to number seventy-nine, the redheaded boy turned to see what was happening. Michael gave him an apologetic look and shrugged his shoulders, but it was evident that the boy had no idea of what had been happening, except that the small, cheeky-looking boy had been sent home. He held Michael's arm for a moment as a gesture of friendliness, waved to the others, and went into his new home.

At the Guests' in number seventy-seven, a cascade of questions descended on the tea table.

"I only hope he didn't hear what Paul said," Eileen commented as she brought in the teapot. "Do you think he is as deaf as all that?"

"He must be as deaf as a post," said Tommy. "He didn't hear a thing when Michael shouted in his ear."

"What I want to know," asked Eileen, "is whether he can talk or not? He said 'Hallo' like anyone else, but nothing more."

"He said, 'Deaf.' "

"Oh, was that what it was? I couldn't make it out."

"Who wants some supper?" called their mother.

"Oh, Mum! I'm starving."

"Eileen, pass the plates through will you? And will you see that Tommy's washed his hands?"

"Mum, can someone who's deaf talk?" asked Tommy.

"Yes, of course. Tommy, what have you been doing? Go and wash at once. And Mike, your hands are none too clean."

Their father came in while Michael and Tommy quarrelled over the soap. Eileen nearly dropped a plate that was too hot: one sausage slipped off, and picking it up she put it back hoping that no one had seen. When they were at last seated at table Tommy asked again:

"Can someone who is deaf talk?"

"What is all this about being deaf?" asked Mrs. Guest.

"It's the boy next door—he can't hear anything," said Michael.

"But he grunts."

"Tommy!"

"But he does."

So they explained all that had happened, and their mother made suitable sympathetic clucking sounds.

"Well, if he is deaf and dumb, he can't talk," she said. "Dumb means silent."

"But——"

"I think they can teach them to talk nowadays," their father said.

"And deaf people usually learn to lip-read," said Mrs. Guest.

"What's that?" asked Tommy.

"By watching the way people's lips move, they can tell what's being said."

"But how could he learn to talk if he doesn't know what it sounds like?" asked Eileen.

"You'd better ask him."

"But, Mum, that's just the point. We *can't* ask him."

"Good heavens! What have I said?" and Mrs. Guest bustled with the teapot, trying to pretend she was not put out by her own stupid remark.

3

* The model village

From the back of the cupboard in his room Michael took a single volume encyclopaedia which he had won as a school prize a couple of years ago. From a diagram in it he had once learnt the deaf and dumb finger alphabet, hoping to use it for passing messages in class; but as no one else had known the signs, his idea had failed. Now he saw he was going to have to relearn it as the only means of talking with this boy.

He sat down on the bed he should have been making, and flicked through the pages. With the illustration on his knees, he laboriously began to memorize the finger alphabet. The vowels were easy: starting with A on the thumb, a finger pointing to each of the successive fingers of the other hand signified E, I, O, and U.

Presently Eileen came upstairs to make her bed.

"I say, Mike, did you see Ted arrive back from his holiday? He's brought a strange girl with him, and his scooter's simply covered with flags and pennants."

"Where's he been?"

"I don't know, but the girl doesn't look more than about fifteen. He must have picked her up somewhere."

"Trust him!"

"Whatever are you doing?"

"Nothing."

"Oh, is that the sign language?"

"Mm."

"Let me see. I want to talk to him, too."

"Oh, all right. You spell your name. No—that's I. No, sorry, you were right. Put your hands down, I can't see."

"But then it's upside down for me."

"No, it isn't. Three fingers is M. N is two. Now spell Guest. That's it. Now our address."

"How do you do figures?"

"I don't know. It doesn't tell you here. Leave them out."

"What's W? Oh, that's like playing, Here's the church, here's the steeple," said Eileen.

Slowly, letter by letter, they spelled out: Windbell Edge Estate.

"Do you mean to say this is the only way we can talk to him?" Eileen asked. "It would be quicker to write it down."

"If he can read and write."

"But, Mike, he must be able to if he can spell."

"Yes, I suppose so. I expect with practice you can get quite quick, like playing the piano or typing."

They spelled out their address a second time, and then Michael remarked:

"You know the queer thing about him is that he doesn't look deaf."

"How do you mean he doesn't look deaf? How could he, anyway?"

"Well," continued Michael, "people who've got something

wrong with them usually show it. If a man's leg's broken, it's in plaster. If he's got a temperature, he looks hot. And anyone can tell a blind man yards away. But this boy—we've no way of knowing he hasn't been having us on."

"Oh, I'm sure he hasn't."

"No, I think he must be totally deaf, but I still——"

A blaring noise from outside brought them both to the window. The boy was sitting on the concrete step outside his front door doing something on a piece of wood, and behind him stood Paul with a sports whistle and Tommy with his toy trumpet.

"We ought to stop them," whispered Eileen, but she was watching the boy's reaction. He continued to cut something with a knife. Paul and Tommy moved a step nearer, and together they blew on the whistle and trumpet another piercing, strident blast. The boy went on placidly whittling with his knife, as though nothing had happened.

"He must have heard that," whispered Eileen incredulously. "He must have."

Paul moved another step nearer, and the boy looked up. While Paul and Tommy stared at him in unexpected embarrassment, he took in what was happening. Gently he shook his head and smiled the curious, apologetic smile they had seen yesterday. As he made a movement towards them, the youngsters backed and fled, suddenly frightened.

Early that morning David had leaned out of the window to look at the view. It was strange and so different from what he had known before: the houses crammed together, the gaunt factories, and shabby sheds which faded as far as one could see into the hazy closeness. Nearby he watched the traffic passing along the main road, the red buses, the loaded lorries, the cars and bicycles.

He saw a garishly colored scooter come down the road and turn into the estate. It was driven by a bareheaded boy, a girl was on the pillion, and the carrier was loaded with luggage. They had obviously come back from a holiday, for a swaying mast was strung with showy pennants. When they dismounted the boy swaggered, and the girl giggled and wobbled on spikey heels as they went into the house.

As David was wondering if they had been to Llandudno, and resolving to have a look at their flags, he felt his mother calling him to breakfast. In their old house his father had fitted a board to the kitchen ceiling below David's room so that she could knock for him without breaking the plaster. Although he could not hear the sound, he could feel the vibrations through the floorboards and in his bones. Now he felt the three knocks through the floor, and ran down to his meal.

His brother Eric was preparing to start off on his new job in a car factory. Their father, too, had already left for a new job as a long-distance lorry driver. David knew that sometimes his father would be away several days at a time, and that he would often be driving all night. It did not occur to him to wonder why they had moved to Blackley, when they had been happy and well settled at Llandudno; and no one had told him the reason.

Ever since he could remember, from the time he was four years old, David had been at a special boarding school for deaf children. This had been necessary for him to get the training he needed, but it also meant that he only saw and lived with his family during the holidays. If, however, his family could settle near a school for the deaf, David would be able to attend as a day-boy, living at home, and so lead a more normal life. There was a deaf school not far from Blackley, to which he could travel each day by bus. So it was largely for David's benefit and pleasure that the family had moved to Windbell Edge.

David spooned up his Cornflakes while his mother hustled Eric off. Presently she came back and sat at the table to speak to him:

"I'm going shopping this morning. Will you be all right by yourself?"

He watched her lips closely, and then nodded and grinned. "See f'en's."

"Good. The people in the next house, I think they're nice. I'll be back about eleven," and she signed the figure to make sure he understood.

When he had finished his meal, David went back upstairs and picked up from the floor a large flat packing case. Carefully he untied the cord that bound it and lifted out the newspaper from inside the top. Underneath were layers of crumpled tissue paper, and finally he took out his most precious possession, to lay it on the bed. Critically he examined his handiwork to make certain that nothing had been broken on the journey.

On a base of plywood he was building a model village, made almost entirely of used matchsticks and glue. The first house he had made was small, with two windows and an open doorway. He had started it last Christmas, and had picked it up again during the Easter holidays, when each of the two succeeding houses had become more elaborate. The second had a detachable roof and a chimney; the third, a door which was hinged on a fine piece of paper, and two rooms inside.

This summer he had begun a row of shops to form the other side of what was going to be the main street. The first two rows of matches, trimmed and cut to size, had been stuck one above the other along the outline of the plan. One was to be a sweet shop, and the foundations of its rooms and even the counter were laid; the second was to be a bicycle shop, and he already had, from a Christmas cracker, a miniature plastic bicycle to be put in the window. He was not sure yet what the third shop was going to be, but the plan was larger than for either of the others.

He carried the board downstairs, and returned to fetch his box of matchsticks, glue, paint, penknife, and odds and ends. Sitting on the front doorstep, he spread his materials around him and began to prepare more matches. The burnt head had to be cut off, and a nick cut at either end, so that each match would dovetail into the other as it was laid.

Pleasantly contented, David sat in the warmth and planned his village. There would have to be a church, but, as the most difficult piece of construction, he was leaving it till the end. A row of houses was to go up beyond the shops; a school farther on; a farm in the corner; a large house with a tower nearby; and there would be a garage by the road.

He was measuring a match to fit one of the shop walls when a shadow fell across the corner of the board, and he looked up to see the two small boys. By their startled expressions he knew they had been blowing the trumpet and whistle at him. He did not mind. He wanted to show them his models, and he was disappointed when they ran away. Turning back he cut the match a fraction of an inch shorter, drew the nozzle of the tube of glue lightly along one side, and stuck it neatly in place. Five minutes later he saw someone else approaching. It was the boy from the next house—the one of about his own age, who looked nice, and who now carried a sheet of paper which appeared to have been torn from a book. David put down the glue and prepared to meet his visitor.

Michael walked up the dazzling concrete path with a hesitant step. The boy smiled at him, and he smiled back. Not knowing what to do next, Michael glanced at the board on the step and saw the models. He squatted down to admire them, and was astonished at their neatness and accuracy.

"I say, did you do all these yourself?" he asked, before he remembered, and, reddening, glanced at the boy. Michael saw that he was almost visibly preening himself at the admiration. Michael took this opportunity to bring out his sheet of paper, and laying it on the ground pointed to the diagram of the finger alphabet. The boy grinned and nodded vigorously. Laboriously Michael misspelled out on his hands:

"W-H-A-T-E-S-Y-U-O-R-N-A-M-E?"

"Davi'wilms."

The loud, uncouth sound shocked Michael. It took him by surprise. Paul was right, he did make noises like an animal.

"Davi'wilms," the boy repeated, making an effort to pronounce his syllables. Michael shook his head.

The boy rummaged in his pockets and brought out a piece of paper from one and a pencil from another. He wrote "David Williams," while Michael sat beside him to read.

"Davi'wilms," he said again, and pointed to his chest. Then he pointed to Michael and looked his question. Michael wrote his name for David to see, and the introduction was complete.

All this time Eileen, Tommy, and Paul had been sitting or standing on the low brick wall that separated the gardens.

"His name's David Williams," Michael called to them. David saw the direction of his glance and smiled. They all came closer. David made a sweeping movement of his arm which indicated the group, and looked enquiringly at Michael. Michael understood, and on the paper he wrote:

"My sister Eileen," and pointed to her.

" 'Allo," said David. He again succeeded in surprising them, though he had said the same word as clearly yesterday.

Michael began to write again but was stopped by David, who pointed to the word "sister" with one hand, and with the other crooked a finger over his nose. Their faces were blank.

"Oh, I've got it," said Eileen as he repeated the movement. "That's a sign for 'sister.' Instead of spelling it out each time you do this." She copied him, and David, pleased that his first lesson had been understood, nodded.

Michael wrote "brother" on the paper, and looked to David for guidance. David rubbed his clenched hands together and then pointed at the word. So Tommy was introduced. Paul's name he could pronounce almost perfectly, that is he said "Paw," but they knew exactly what he meant. He knew that Paul lived in the house on the other side, and asked by signs if he had any brothers or sisters. Paul shook his head. David then made the brother sign, clasped one hand to his chest, and lifted the other above his head. They stared at him, and he repeated the movements more slowly, but they could not follow what he was trying to say. He reached for the pencil and paper and wrote: "I have big brother Eric."

This led to David teaching them the signs for father and mother, which were the F and M of the finger alphabet, and then those for other members of the family. By now Tommy and Paul had become tired and drifted away. It had been fun at first, but it was all too slow, and it looked as though David would go on indefinitely.

Some time later, when David was trying to explain that he came from Llandudno, there came a call from across the grass:

"Michael. Mike."

"What?" he yelled back.

"Come and play cricket."

"Can't you manage without me?"

"No."

"Hang on. I'll be with you in a minute."

He wrote that he had to go. Eileen remembered she still had not made her bed, so their lesson broke up.

Michael was relieved, because it had been a strain to keep up with David's mixture of signs and writing; but he also hoped that David was not offended that they had all run away.

If David had known what it was to whistle, or hum, he would now have been whistling away cheerily, for he was entirely happy. It was not often he had the chance of talking to people of his own age who were not themselves deaf. It was something of a triumph that he had succeeded at all.

Now a whole family had, of their own accord, come to make friends with him. This had never happened to him before, and if Eileen and Michael could have known they might have stayed a little longer. But David was satisfied. He turned back to his matches and models, and planned a large castle to go in the corner: a castle with turrets, and towers, battlements, and a bridge that would lift up and down. He would make guns and perhaps the used match heads would do for shot. He did not know the words drawbridge and cannon, but he planned and dreamed.

Across the grass Michael made up a team of some half-dozen boys to play cricket. While he stood fielding, he told them something of David. They were curious about the boy, and assumed that, because he was deaf and dumb, he was simple.

"But he's not dumb," Michael insisted. "He can say a few words—at least if you can understand them."

"Oh, go on," said the wicketkeeper as he tossed the ball back. "They always are peculiar, you know that. He's plain nuts."

The batsman hit the ball in Michael's direction and he ran to field it.

"He's not nuts," he told the wicketkeeper when he got back into position. "He's making a smashing model out of matchsticks."

"Anyone can stick a few matches together."

"They aren't just stuck. He's making a good job of it."

"You're soft about him."

"Look out, he's bowling."

The wicketkeeper jumped behind the stumps, but the batsman hit the ball squarely and upwards. Michael ran for the catch and held it. It was now his turn to bat.

He was feeling annoyed with the wicketkeeper, who had not seen David's models or his welcoming smile when Michael had approached him, and he was not going to allow him the pleasure of stumping him out. So he began to hit firmly at the ball. He hit a couple for which the fielders had to run, but he missed the next ball which almost scraped the stumps. The fourth ball was wide, but an easy one to hit, so he stepped out and gave it a swipe. It swung high across the grass, bounced on the road, and into one of the gardens.

"A boundary!" someone called.

"It nearly smashed a window."

Two of the fielders raced to fetch the ball and called to the boy who was sitting at the door to throw it back. Only then did Michael realize that it had landed in David's garden.

"He can't hear you," he cried, but they took no notice.

"Hey! Throw it back, can't you?"

"I'll get it," said Michael, and began to walk across.

David was sitting with his back towards them, so could not have seen what had happened. Michael noticed that he was sitting still, unnaturally still. Had the ball hit him? Michael slowed down and looked more closely.

"But he's sitting up. If he'd been knocked out, he'd be lying down." He walked on, but David had not moved.

Sensing that something was wrong, the other boys followed Michael. They too saw how rigidly David was sitting.

Michael reached the pavement and stopped by the wall.

The ball was lying by the doorstep, so David must have seen it, but his eyes were fixed on his models. As Michael's glance followed that of David's he knew what had happened. The whole row of three houses which David had spent weeks in building were lying flat and splintered. Bits of matches gleamed white and raw where the paintwork was torn, and whole walls had been flung apart.

A row of boys now stood by the wall, watching the motionless David.

"Oh, go on," said one of them. "It's only matches. They can easily be stuck together again. What's all the fuss about?"

"Shut up," said another. "The kid's crying."

"What'll we do now?"

Seeing a crowd by the gate, other children joined the group. The boy who had been playing wicketkeeper prodded Michael and said:

"You know how to talk to him. Go and get the ball back and say you're sorry."

"Yes, you go, Mike," and he was pushed unwillingly towards the path.

"But I couldn't explain all that."

"Well, you're the only one he knows."

"Go on, Mike. It'll have to be you," and he was pushed a bit farther.

"But I can't. He wouldn't understand, and I don't know the signs."

By this time Eileen had joined the crowd, and Tommy and Paul were running down the garden to see what was happening. Eileen made the most practical suggestion.

"Why not see if his mother's in? At least we could explain to her it was an accident."

"Suppose she's deaf, too?"

"No, she isn't. I saw her talking to Paul's mother yesterday."

They would probably have tried to carry out this suggestion, if David had not looked up. He saw Michael, without recognizing him: he was standing in front of what appeared to be a large crowd; and he was carrying a cricket bat. David let out a wailing cry and sprang upon him. So unexpected was the assault and so wild its fury that Michael was thrown to the ground before anyone realized what had happened. David sat astride him and with his clenched fists hit wildly at whatever part of Michael's body happened to be nearest.

It took a few moments for everyone to recover from the surprise of the attack, but soon half a dozen boys were picking David off. They tried to catch his swinging arms, but found they were clutching each other. They tripped over Michael's body and fell in a pile. David started to kick wildly and blindly in every direction. Slowly Michael managed to wriggle free and held one of David's legs. Someone else gripped the other, and presently David was pinned to the ground. He lay panting and staring. He looked at Michael and recognized him; but then with a sudden, quick twist of his body he sprang free of his captors, scrambled to his feet, and ran sobbing into the house.

"The little spitfire!" someone murmured from the crowd.

They disentangled themselves and pulled their shirts straight. Michael licked a graze on the back of his hand.

Ted strolled unnoticed towards them with the unknown girl hanging on his arm. Ted was feared by those boys who were younger than he for he did not hesitate to use the force of his fists and arms when he thought it necessary.

"What's the to-do?" he asked in a voice that was patronizing. "If anyone needs walloping send them along to me."

No one answered.

"Oh, Ted, it wouldn't be fair for you to hit kids like these," said the girl, admiringly. Visibly basking in her gaze Ted swaggered as they walked on towards the main road.

Michael went to the front door and squatted to inspect the damage done to David's models. It was not as bad as he had feared. One of the houses was completely smashed and would have to be rebuilt; and the walls of the other two had been broken apart from each other, but the individual matches had remained stuck together. These could easily be fitted into place again, though part of the roofs would have to be rebuilt.

"What's it like?" asked one of the boys, and he, too, came to have a look. There was a general drift up the path; but, as sobs were heard from inside the house, the boys stopped to glance nervously at the windows.

"Look out!" cried Paul from the road. "His mother's coming back."

Within seconds the crowd was dispersed. Most of them disappeared over the fence to the shelter of the Bank behind. The Bank was a mound built from the waste of one of the old coal mines, now disused. Covered with coarse grass and small mallow bushes it served as a meeting place, fort, or hiding place as required, and soon the boys were scattered behind its sheltering slopes and making their way up to the hill above.

Michael remained where he was. If anyone could help to put this right and explain to David what had happened, it would surely be his mother. David's great gulping sobs had died down, but Michael could hear that he was still crying. He glanced again at the broken models, and looked up to see that Mrs. Williams was approaching across the grass. Would she be angry, or would she understand? She might easily think the crowd of boys she must have seen running away had been baiting her son.

Suddenly frightened, Michael picked up the cricket ball, and slipped across to his own garden.

4

* Eric explains

All that afternoon Michael mooned about the house and down by the canal. He tried throwing stones at a tin floating on the far side, but could not hit it. He kicked a stick into the water, and in doing so stubbed a toe on a stone.

"Blast!"

He strode off, along the canal path in the hope that something might happen, but he reached the tunnel without meeting anyone, or seeing anything of interest.

The canal which ran along the hillside below the estate was one of a whole network which had been built long ago to link the new factories of the Industrial Revolution with the seaports and the rest of the country. The Blackley Canal was one of a number which linked the Birmingham area with the Severn valley and Bristol. In order to reach Birmingham it had been necessary to cut a tunnel nearly a mile and a half long under Windbell Edge; and it was at its dark entrance that Michael now stood.

As usual and in spite of the notice forbidding entry to "any unauthorized person," Michael walked a short way in along the towpath which clung to one wall. He peered through the darkness to the tiny circle of light which indicated the other end, but which was too far away to be distinguishable as more than a blob. Shivering in the chilliness, he soon turned back to the daylight behind him, and climbed the steep cutting to sit in the grass above.

"Blast!" he said to himself. "Blast!"

It had been Eileen who had thought of writing a letter. If he had thought of it himself, he would have written it by now, but he was reluctant to admit that her suggestion was the best. Instead, he had spent the afternoon trying to think of another way of telling David he was sorry; but he had been unable to find a better method. Probably David was thinking he had thrown the ball on purpose.

Seeing no other way round the problem, Michael stood up and made his way home at last. In the kitchen he found two used matches, but his father's ash tray had been cleaned and he could find no others. He wandered down to the first shop in the village and bought a box. Then again he sat by the canal and began to strike them one by one, blowing them out before they had burnt too far. Presently he was striking three or four together to get through them faster, and he enjoyed watching the explosive flame. This at least was his own idea.

Back in his room and feeling happier he wrote a brief note to David, explaining what had happened and offering to help him to mend the models. He made a parcel of the matches and note together, and ran out to push them through David's letterbox before anyone had time to see him.

They saw nothing of David for the rest of that day, but during the evening David's brother, Eric, knocked at the open kitchen door.

"Hallo," he said. "I'm from next door. Is young Michael about?"

"I think he's up the garden somewhere," said Mrs. Guest. "Eileen, go and fetch him. You must be David's brother."

"Yes, that's right. I thought I'd come round and try to straighten out a few things."

"Michael was terribly upset about breaking his models."

"We thought as much, but he mustn't take it too hardly. David's already got over it. Hallo, Michael. I'm Eric."

"Hallo," said Michael, as he came in with some hesitation.

"I've just come to thank you for your letter to David, and I thought I'd explain a few things at the same time."

"Will he let me help mend the models?"

"Yes, that's a good idea, though I don't suppose he'll actually let you do much."

"Why?"

"He likes to do it all himself, and he hates anybody messing it up, as he thinks."

"How much can he talk?" asked Eileen, "and can he lip-read? He doesn't seem to understand us at all."

"Well, I was going to ask you all, especially Michael, if you could help him a bit."

"Help him? How?"

"Sit down," said Mrs. Guest, "and we'll have some tea. Eileen, put the kettle on and get out those buns, and there's some biscuits in the red tin. I think it's such a shame David should be like that, and so terrible for your poor mother to have a boy who isn't quite right."

Eric sighed as Mrs. Guest bustled about. It was always the same: people would not understand that the deaf only appeared to be "not quite right," and that they were ordinary human beings who needed more help than most. He could see that Mrs. Guest was going to be difficult to convince, but he looked for understanding in Michael.

"You know, Michael," he said as they sat round the kitchen table, "you could be one of the best things that's happened to David, if you wanted to be."

"How do you mean?"

"He's never had any hearing friends of his own age, and he doesn't know how to mix with people. It's difficult enough as it is for him, even amongst his own family and at school, but it's very much worse among people who don't know his limitations."

"It's difficult for us, too."

"Yes, I know. Look, I think I'd better start at the beginning. David was born deaf but it wasn't discovered until he was nearly three years old and hadn't begun to talk. You see, he made all the usual baby noises. He cried and gurgled, and so on, so that no one knew anything was wrong. It's quite natural to giggle, laugh with happiness, or yell with fright, just as one would yawn or cry. None of these need language. It's language that has to be learnt by ear. That's what is so difficult for the severely deaf: though many of them learn to read and write normally, only a few learn to speak well enough to be understood.

"Normal babies are hearing sounds all the time. They hear the sound of a spoon on a plate, and so they know it's feeding time. They hear people talk—they hear their names being called, and so learn that the name belongs to them. But as a baby David never heard a single human voice—ever; so he couldn't develop a normal voice of his own. He made up for this by using his eyes more keenly. When he saw the spoon in his plate he knew it was meal time, and when he saw Mother hold out her hand to him he came running to take it. Oh, and lots of little things like that.

"But by the time he was three, he didn't even know he had a name of his own, and he didn't know that such simple words as 'yes' or 'no' existed. His deafness was discovered because he hadn't begun to talk at all and, of course, he was already behind in learning the usual things. It takes too long to explain how he was taught, but the idea is that he was encouraged to watch our lips when we spoke to him."

"Then he can lip-read," said Michael.

"Yes, but lip-reading's not as easy as all that. David can usually do it only for people he knows well. And don't forget, he can only lip-read the words he happens to know."

"Fancy!" said Mrs. Guest, and suddenly realizing the kettle was boiling, she jumped up to make the tea.

"Do you talk to him as you do to us?" asked Michael. "Or do you shout, or only move your lips and pretend to speak?"

"No, it's most important to talk perfectly normally. For heaven's sake don't start making faces at him, or he won't get a thing, and he'll think you're making fun of him. It's best to use easy words and fairly short sentences, and after a time you'll find he's beginning to understand you, or at least picking out a word or two."

"But what about all the rest?"

"Well, you'll gradually pick up the signs and alphabet, but at the moment I should write down what he doesn't understand."

"But it's so slow and complicated."

"I know. Unfortunately, people seem to think that, as soon as the deaf learn to lip-read, all the problems are solved. That may be true of those who are only partially deaf—'partially deaf' and 'severely deaf' are the official descriptions of some of the degrees of deafness. Many people who are only partially deaf can help themselves a great deal by lip-reading, especially if they have learnt enough of the language to know the more difficult words. But with many as deaf as David—severely deaf, that is—lip-reading doesn't solve everything. David will probably always have to use some signs and writing. I'm afraid you'll need to be patient with him."

"Can't he hear anything at all?" asked Eileen. "Even a train roaring through a station, or—or something like that?"

"Hardly. At least he can hear certain notes when they're played to him through a special hearing aid. They did that at his deaf school; but it's not much practical use to him. He's never heard anyone speak."

"But how does he learn to talk?" asked Michael. "And some things he says are quite clear and others we can't make out at all."

"Some sounds are more difficult to make. He'll probably show you some of the tricks himself, but basically he is taught to feel the vibrations in his throat and mouth and on his lips."

"Well," said Mrs. Guest, "I had no idea it was all so difficult as that. It's no wonder he gets wild at times."

"He doesn't often have an outburst like this morning's, but every now and again things get a bit too much for him and he can't express himself any other way. It's a terrible strain, you know, all the time. But don't worry about it, Michael. Your letter put everything straight. Why don't you come over tomorrow and give him a hand with the repairs?"

"Yes, I will."

When Michael went to bed that night he could not sleep. For probably the first time he consciously lay and listened for all the sounds he could hear. First, he noticed the obvious noises from the town: the traffic, sometimes close and distinguishable, sometimes distant and merged into a continuous hum; the steam hammer still beating steadily and rhythmically; the clanking of trucks in the goods yard; the barking of a dog; and voices from some house not far away.

Then he listened to the sounds from within his own home. When he moved, the springs in the mattress creaked, and the bedclothes rustled. His mother walked from the kitchen to the sitting room: he knew it was she by her step. There was the clink of china on the hearth to tell him that his parents were having their late evening drink. He heard his father strike a match, and if he could not actually hear him drawing on his pipe, he knew how it would sound. He waited for another match to be struck, and timed it almost to the second.

He moved his head slightly and heard his hair brush across the pillow.

He pushed a finger in each ear, and, though the outside noises were blocked, there was a humming that was almost louder than anything else. If he bent each finger backwards and forwards the noise increased, and he could only describe it to himself as the movement of the muscles, or sinews, or joints, or perhaps all three.

He lay back and put his arms behind his head. The clock in the sitting room chimed the quarters, and as the eleven strokes beat out he heard them, but at the same time he felt a new sensation: the vibrations through the headboard and on his arms.

Of course, Michael had learned about sound vibrations in his physics lessons; had watched the tuning fork and the plucked string bouncing backwards and forwards, and had listened to a watch ticking from the other end of the bench; but he never before remembered having *felt* sound.

5

✻ *"Watch"*

Next morning Michael went round to all his friends and collected as many used matches as he could persuade them to find. One or two boys promised to keep more for him in the future. He knocked at David's kitchen door, beyond which he could hear his mother mixing something in a basin.

"Hallo," said Mrs. Williams. "You must be Michael. David's in the front room. Would you like to go through and find him? I'll bring you something to eat presently, but I must finish this."

David was sitting at the table with his back to the door. The board with the models was in front of him, and he was preparing more matches. He did not see Michael come in, so Michael went round the table and stood at one side. David looked up with a wide grin on his face, and it was hard to believe that he was capable of losing his temper.

"Here are some more matches," said Michael self-consciously, for it seemed illogical to speak aloud.

"Thahnkoo." And Michael wondered why they had not noticed yesterday how flat and expressionless David's voice was.

David looked into the paper bag, nodded, and tipped the contents into a box already half full of used matches. Michael sat down to inspect the damage more closely, but David had stripped the broken models off the board. He touched David's arm to attract his attention and asked:

"What are you doing?" As David did not understand, Michael took out the paper and pencil he had been careful to bring, and wrote the question down, adding: "Can I help?"

"Wash," said David.

"What?"

"Wash. Wash."

Michael shook his head, and David took up the pencil.

"Watch," he wrote. So Michael sat and watched him trimming matches, gluing, and sticking them together. He was rebuilding the whole of each house, having discarded those walls which had remained in one piece, and presently Michael saw the reason for this. Each match was cut and dovetailed at the corners of the model to give the effect of a log cabin, and the broken walls, though each in one piece, were twisted and would not fit.

Michael assumed David would give him something to do later, so for a while he sat happily. He noticed that David was now showing off. That did not worry him, for after all David had something well worth showing off; but gradually Michael realized he was going to have to play the part of an audience for the rest of the morning. He began to fidget, and while David was using the glue, he picked up the knife to trim a match. As soon as David saw this, he snatched the knife back and clasped it against his chest.

"Gosh!" thought Michael. "He's like a kid who won't share his toys."

He watched David trim a match to the exact size to fit a small space, cutting tiny chips from each end, and he knew his own fingers were too clumsy to do it as well. He sat back and contemplated the board. In spite of the skill with which the models were made, it looked bare and empty. It needed some greenery, trees and hedges.

Mrs. Williams came in with a plate of gingerbread and glasses of orange juice. She cleared a pile of linen from a chair and sat down to talk for a while.

"David, let Michael help;" and Michael noticed that in order to watch his mother's lips, David had to stop using his hands; but he understood what she was saying, and shook his head.

"I'm sorry, Michael. We shouldn't have let him get like this over his models, but he sets great store by them. He's not as bad over his other things. The trouble is we've spoilt him a bit. If he'd been nearer Eric's age, or had had a younger brother he'd have to share his things more."

When Mrs. Williams had left them, Michael asked David what else he was planning to build. David sketched lightly in pencil the ground plans of the school, church, houses, garage, and castle. Michael thought he would practice the finger alphabet, so he spelt out:

"Y-E-A-R-S-O-F-W-O-R-K."

David grinned. Michael sat back again and was soon as bored as before. He picked a crumb of gingerbread off the table and drained the last drop of orange juice. Soon he reached for the paper and pencil and scribbled:

"I'll be back in a minute."

He ran home, rummaged for his paint-box, raided the medicine chest for a packet of cotton wool, and returned to David. He asked Mrs. Williams for a jar of water, and intrigued David by refusing to tell him what he was going to do.

"Watch," was all he would say, and he had a sense of satisfaction when he saw that David had read the word on his lips.
First he mixed some good, thick green paint. He tore off a
number of blobs of cotton wool, dipped them in the paint,
squeezed the water out, and set them in the sun to dry. Then
he borrowed the knife to cut a point at each end of a number
of matchsticks. With a bradawl he found among the tools, he
made some holes in the board behind one of the cottages, and
glued the matches upright in them.

David guessed what they were to be, and made some fast
movements with his fingers. Excitedly he repeated the movements, but Michael made him repeat them again slowly until
he could see the word "trees" spelt out.

The blobs of cotton wool had hardly dried. They were paler
than Michael had intended, and he had forgotten how much
cotton wool shrinks when wet; but they would do. Together
they fixed them on top of the matches. David had an even
better idea. He split a match down half its length, bent one
half outwards to form a branch, and fixed a blob of cotton wool
on each prong. Then with some red paint he flecked the tree
with flowers.

They stood back to admire the effect. David clutched Michael's arm, and began to laugh out loud. Soon they were both
rolling about the room in fits of giggles, for their trees looked
like nothing more than wet, bedraggled, green feathers, the
kind used for trimming hats. Michael plucked one from the
board and stuck it in his hair. He stood back to pull an imagi-
nary bow, and was Robin Hood. David roared and rolled into
an armchair.

Mrs. Williams came in, and behind her were Tommy and
Paul, clearly puzzled. It came as something of a shock to them
to see and hear David laughing in a normal, healthy way.

With a mixture of signs, mime, and speech that was unintelligible to all but Mrs. Williams, David tried to explain what had happened. At the appropriate point Michael took up his stance and drew his bow. Either the boys did not see the joke, or more probably had not followed all that David was trying to tell them; the performance could not draw more than puzzled smiles of sympathy mixed with pity.

"Michael, your brother's come to fetch you for lunch," said Mrs. Williams.

"All right, I'm coming." He pulled the matchstick and cotton wool from his hair, and was moving to the door. Then he reached for the paper and pencil.

"I'll find a way to make them come out better," he wrote, and passed the message to David. To his surprise David did not understand. He puzzled over the words and then wrote:

"Where are you going?"

"Home to dinner."

Michael wondered why David still looked bewildered. He was after all a bit odd, for Michael had written only two simple sentences that he must have understood.

David picked up the pencil and in Michael's original sentence underlined the words "find a way," and "come out."

"For crying out loud!" exclaimed Michael. "He's taken me word for word." After a moment's thought he wrote:

"I'll make better trees next time."

David grinned and put up both his thumbs.

By the end of the week David had rebuilt the three houses even more neatly than the originals, for he had now acquired greater skill. He had left the roofs loose, so that they could be lifted off to see the interiors. Michael had tried various ways of improving the trees. He swapped a ball-point pen for a pot of dark green poster-paint, which produced a more substantial color; but he had difficulty in making the cotton wool, even when dry, look remotely like clusters of leaves. It was his mother's suggestion to add some starch to the paint, to use a much larger piece of cotton wool, and then to model the still damp mass into whatever shape he wanted, as he might have done with clay or plasticine. When the shapes dried they did not fluff out but remained firm. From his encyclopaedia he found illustrations of various kinds of trees, and using these as a pattern built up pines, yews, a cedar, and poplar trees. By using grains of rice to represent flowers he made a horse chestnut which became the pride of the collection.

When the repairs were complete and the miniature forest planted behind the cottage gardens, Michael brought some of his friends to see the results. The boys were more impressed than they had expected to be. One of them remarked:

"He's not nearly so dumb as he sounds."

6

* Summer friendship

Michael had promised to show David the canal and to take him over the hill. Eileen said she would come with them; and, it being Sunday, Eric was free to join the party as well. Paul and Tommy followed behind.

David had never seen a canal before, and had taken the strip of water to be a river. He called it the Canal, thinking the word was a name, and using it as one would "the Thames," or "the Conway"—which he had known near Llandudno. Michael found it more difficult than he thought possible to explain the meaning to him. With amusement Eric watched him miming the action of digging a trench, pouring water into it, and then trying to imitate a boat sailing along.

"You won't do it that way," said Eric. "You look as though you're running an obstacle race without any obstacles, or trying to be a duck swimming in custard. Here, let me show him."

So they sat by the towpath and with a mixture of finger-spelling, signs, lip-reading, and diagrams, Eric explained the meaning of the word. Eileen was impressed both by the patience he had with his brother, and by the enormous difficulty of trying to convey the full meaning of what at first sight was a simple word.

She asked:

"However does he learn anything at school? It must take ages and ages."

"Yes, it does," replied Eric. "I don't know how they do it myself, but there are a few tricks—like learning the sounds of letters." He touched David on the shoulder to draw his attention. "Show us how you learnt to say P."

David picked a blade of grass and held it in front of his lips. As he repeatedly said "Pe,pe,pe,pe," the little explosive breath which escaped from between his slightly opened lips blew the grass forward. Eileen tried the experiment, and Michael asked:

"But how does he know he's making a sound, or can he hear himself?"

"No, he can't hear himself, but he can feel it." Eric signed something to David, and for reply David picked up Michael's hand and held it against his own cheek. First David opened and shut his mouth without making any sound, and Michael could feel his jaw moving up and down. He then began to utter some noises, which to Michael at least were unintelligible, and Michael himself could not follow what was happening or what he was supposed to understand.

Again David, still pressing Michael's hand to his cheek, moved his mouth mechanically and without making a sound. He did this a number of times before speaking again, or rather uttering a prolonged "Ah" which might have been a howl or a hum.

"Feel it?" asked Eric.

Michael shook his head. Feel it? Feel what? He pressed his fingers on David's cheek and felt his jawbone and his teeth. At last as David repeated the noise, he began to feel the slight tingling at his finger tips.

"Oh, I've got it. It's the sound vibrations. But they're very faint."

"You're not used to it yet," said Eric. "Try on his throat; it may be stronger."

Michael placed his hand across David's throat, and as David obligingly continued to make noises, he felt the vibrations more clearly.

All this time Eileen, Paul, and Tommy had been watching. The younger boys hardly understood the experiment, but it was one more strange manifestation of this strange boy. Soon they were clamoring to try the new game for themselves, and Eric suggested they felt each other's throats and cheeks. To their untutored and insensitive fingers there was often nothing to feel at all. They tried different kinds of sounds, finding that some produced stronger vibrations on the cheeks, others in the throat. A gentle hum made with the mouth closed produced one of the strongest sensations to be felt through the cheeks.

"Let's get moving," said Michael at last. "The canal tunnel's only round the corner."

Eric and David were impressed by the tunnel. Though Michael explained that there was little traffic on the canal now, they lingered in the hope of seeing one of the narrow boats come through. But at last they left, to climb to the top of Windbell Edge. They walked across to a vantage point where they could see most of Birmingham laid out before them; gray, murky, and fading into the haze. Eric searched the area in which his factory lay, and Michael pointed out the district where David's new school was.

The beginning of August found most of the families of the estate cheerfully and noisily setting off on their summer holidays at the seaside. But the Guests could not afford a holiday this year. Tommy was sent to spend a week with some cousins in the country, but Michael and Eileen stayed at home. They were thrown into each other's company, and had to rely largely on David for some of their amusement. They found him to be cheerful, easygoing, and willing, so far as he was able, to join in their exploits. He was fond of going to the cinema and spent most of his pocket money in this way. During these weeks Michael went with him to show him where the cinemas were, and they saw four films within ten days, until Michael said he had spent all his money.

The cinema and television were David's substitute for adventure books. While he could watch the action, he need not try to lip-read the characters on the screen; and, though he could read easy stories, it was less of a strain to watch the action being performed. But it was all very boring for Michael. He enjoyed the first two films, but by the third he was regretting the sun outside and the hill behind their home. The cinema was for the winter, not a hot August holiday.

Then there were the buses. Michael himself was becoming used to David's silences, his occasional toneless and loud speech, and his signs, but it was embarrassing when a bus full of women going to the shops had nothing better to do for the moment than to stare. No one noticed the boys when they boarded the bus or when Michael paid their fares, but as soon as David made a sign or noise, curious glances were aimed at them. Sometimes a small child would nudge his mother for an explanation, only to be given a command to keep quiet. Michael asked David if he minded people staring at him. David did not know the word stare, and Michael crossed it out and substituted "look at."

"No. Do you?" was David's quick retort, and Michael could only agree that he did not mind either.

The cinema seemed the easiest way of making a companion of David, for there was no need to talk. If they went along the canal or up the hill together, the walk was almost silent, and Michael felt he might have enjoyed himself more on his own. While they were walking, David could not watch his lip movements, and Michael's use of the finger alphabet was not nearly fluent enough for conversation. For what little there was for them to say, they had to stop, and find some spot where they could rest their scraps of writing paper—a wall, a flat stone, or sometimes their bare knees.

Clearly David enjoyed these tramps. He seemed fascinated by the factories that could be seen from the hillside and wanted to know what each of them produced. Once when they were returning from a walk beyond the canal and were strolling down a quiet street near the iron works, David suddenly stopped and placed his hands flat against the blackened brick wall which bordered the pavement. Only when he lifted one arm and beat time to the rhythm of the steam hammer did Michael realize what he was doing. Michael was so used to the sound that he was rarely conscious of it; David must have felt the beating through the pavement, and had used his hands to get a clearer impression. David wanted an explanation, and Michael made an involved series of diagrams and notes. But it was impossible to know how much David had understood.

It was not surprising that, as his friends came back from holiday, Michael turned to them with relief. He could crack a joke before it lost its point from the laborious method of writing down or spelling out on his fingers. He joined a crowd of boys who were planning to build a raft to float on the canal, and left David on his own.

"After all," Michael told himself, "he won't really let me help with his modelling, and he can make the trees as well as I can now, so he might as well get on with it. And he can always go to the pictures with Eric in the evenings."

7

* *A sporting chance*

One Saturday morning brought a break in the long dusty spell that so many families had enjoyed for their summer holidays. Most of them were back from their two weeks by the sea, and could watch the rain streaming against the windows with the knowledge that they had had the best of the summer.

David sat happily with his models, which he had neglected for the past few weeks. He pencilled in the ground plan of a school, and marked the places for miniature desks and tables. He drew in the playground, gate, and the schoolhouse beyond, and then he started to trim, glue, and lay the matches.

By lunch time the rain had stopped, the dark clouds gave way to light billowing ones, and patches of blue sky appeared. After his meal David decided to find Michael and ask him to come out. To avoid the slow process of finger-spelling, he had invented a sign for Michael's name: he outlined with his finger a curly shape on his forehead to imitate the curl which would fall forward over Michael's eyes.

Eileen answered the door and explained as best she could that Michael had gone with one of his friends to watch the first soccer match of the season. David lingered a moment, hoping that Eileen would ask him in, but she was busy washing up and did not seem disposed to give him her attention. This was not intended unkindness on Eileen's part, for she did not know how intensely David was longing for companionship. Though he was used to his own company, there were times, especially during the holidays, when he felt very much alone.

David walked slowly towards the grass by the swings. The fresh cool breeze after the rain reminded him of the sea. He had a longing to run splashing into the waves. He wanted to run: to run across the sands, or to skip surefootedly over boulders; but all that was offered him were streets and pavements and the patch of moth-eaten looking grass. He played with the idea of walking up Windbell Edge, but would have liked someone to come with him.

Beyond the swings Ted was partially dismantling his scooter and appeared to be taking bits from its engine. David strolled across to watch.

Ted's girl friend had been showing an interest in Eric, so Ted was jealous of the good-looking newcomer. The last thing he wanted was to have Eric's young brother, handicapped though he was, hanging around and being inquisitive. He pretended not to see David, and pointedly turned his back.

David watched for a while, assuming that Ted was shy of speaking to him, but at last he sensed he was not welcome. He turned to relieve his feelings on one of the swings, pushing it as high as he dared. He swung until his head began to feel dizzy and then allowed his weight alone to keep the dying momentum going awhile.

Presently a crowd of boys ran on to the grass with a football.

They fixed up temporary goal posts of sticks and jackets, and after some argument divided themselves into teams according to size and age. David was quick to notice they were an un-even number; but though they must have seen him on the swing, they did not ask him to join them. Paul and Tommy were among them, and David wondered if he could catch their attention.

He watched the game for ten minutes, kicking his heels into the ground beneath the swing, before his opportunity came. Tommy failed to stop the ball, and it came rolling down the slight slope towards the swings: David picked it up. He approached Tommy as he came to collect it. He pointed to himself, the ball, and the players, to ask if he could join in.

"He wants to play with us," Tommy called over his shoul-der.

"Can he play soccer?" one of them asked, as though there was some doubt of David's ability to understand the game.

"Oh, I expect so," Tommy asked. "Shall we let him?"

"All right," cried the leader of Tommy's team. "We're one short, so we'll give him a try." He beckoned to David, who ran happily to join them.

At first they were polite and allowed him a fair share of the ball, and he in turn was determined to please. They soon found he was a practiced player, and the game livened. David was supremely happy: for the first time since he could remember, he was playing an equal part in a game with almost unknown hearing boys, and he was going to show them he was every bit as good as they were. At least four of the boys were about his age, and one looked older; Paul and Tommy were the only youngsters.

At last David was enjoying the freshness of the afternoon, the wind tingling against his bare arms and cheeks; and the sun that was now shining in an almost clear sky brought out the smell of damp earth and grass. He chased after the ball as though he were in practice for a Cup Final, and when not running flexed his muscles by prancing up and down.

As his spirits rose higher, David unconsciously took charge of the game. He kept the ball longer than he should, failed to pass it to Tommy to give him a fair share, and gradually was playing both forward and back. He saved a goal which the goalkeeper would have liked to stop, and he then dribbled the ball up the field, maneuvered round an opponent, sidestepped Paul, and shot a goal for his team. He looked round to see what effect his playing had created, and mistook the looks of surprise for praise rather than condemnation.

"You'd think he was playing by himself," was one comment.

"Doesn't he know how to play fair?" was another.

In their turn the other boys mistook David's playing for showing-off rather than for high spirits. They could not know that when he played at school with other boys who were as deaf or nearly as deaf as himself, David played with fair teamwork. Now his action became not only another example of his strangeness, but was also called mean. The boys' immediate reaction was to keep the ball away from him; and, as the game continued, David found he was following the ball and not playing with it.

When a pass was made to Tommy, he ran to intercept it and again had the ball.

"Hey! Give the kid a chance!" someone called out.

As David dribbled the ball up the field and Paul prepared to tackle him, a new voice came from the sidelines, for Ted had joined the small audience that was gathering.

"Go on, Paul. Tackle him good and proper, and I'll give you a scooter ride," Ted called, seeing an opportunity of getting his own back on Eric.

"Go on, tackle him!" The cry was taken up by others, but

David outpaced Paul and before anyone else could tackle him he slipped the ball to one of his teammates. The moment passed, and David again found himself left without the ball. In a slack moment he saw the audience of boys around and grew more determined than before to show them he could play. When the ball was headed from one end of the pitch, David ran towards the point where it would drop, and in the concentration of looking upwards did not see that Tommy was also trying to reach it. Being that much taller, David took the pass, and not until he had knocked Tommy over did he realize that anyone else was near him.

"Oh, shame!" called one of the players.

"Boo-oo!"

In a glance David saw that Tommy was unharmed and already getting to his feet, so he took the ball to dribble up the field.

"Go on, Paul," said Ted's urgent voice. "Go on and get your revenge."

Paul charged ferociously, partly because the whole spirit of the game had changed and partly because he had long wanted a ride on Ted's scooter. With his head down he rammed David's waist and flung him to the ground, winded.

David lay recovering his breath, and watched the legs and feet gathering round him. Presently he managed to look up and gave a weak smile, but no one responded and no one helped him to his feet: they were discussing him among themselves.

"How do we talk to him?"

"Tommy knows."

"Mike does. I can only do a few finger letters. You can write everything down and he'll read it."

"That's too complicated."

"Where's Mike?"

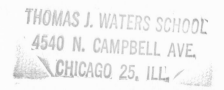

"Gone to watch the match."

"Well, how can we tell him he's got to learn to play properly?"

"I don't know."

"And he's a show-off."

"And a cheat. He took the ball from me twice."

"He's a coot, mad, soft, dumb."

They were ganging up against the stranger, an interloper. None of the boys wished to seem unsympathetic, but David had offended against their laws of fair play, and they did not know what to do about it. They stood facing him, someone who could not hear a single word they wanted to say. They were baffled by the barrier of silence. Instinctively drawing together, they bolstered each other up with words they would never have used if David could have heard them. He could not hear them. All the time this was nagging, hammering through their minds. He can't hear. He can't hear. He makes noises like an animal.

Because they could not understand their own uncomfortable feelings, they became suspicious and afraid: suspicious of him and afraid of themselves.

Few people realize that though the deaf are taught to lip-read, lip-reading in itself is not only a difficult art to acquire but is also highly inaccurate. Lips formed to the same shape or making the same movements can produce different sounds. The sounds of T, D, and N are very different when spoken and heard, but the movements made by the lips to produce them are almost the same. If someone says "toe" the deaf person watching his lips has to guess whether it may be "toe," "doe," "dough," or "no." To anyone who cannot hear there is no way of knowing what some words may be, except by the general sense of the conversation.

Another habit of some deaf people is that they tend to ignore small words. The effort of lip-reading is such a strain that only the main words of a sentence may be picked out and the rest allowed to pass or to be guessed. When, in a difficult situation, one is desperately trying to translate the slight and subtle flapping, pouting, stretching, opening, and shutting of lips into meaning, words like "a," "the," "in," or "on" are relatively unimportant.

As David sat up and saw the boys around him talking, he looked from face to face trying to decipher what the fuss was about. They appeared to be angry. Was it with Paul for having knocked him down? He picked the face that was nearest him and which he could see most clearly. He watched the rapidly moving lips, desperately trying to read a sentence or even catch a word.

He saw the very slight heave of the chest for an aspirate, followed by the narrowly opened lips of the long E sound, and the drawing together to make an S—"He's." The next important word seemed easy—"Good."

The only phrase he was able to lip-read had been, in fact, "He's a coot." David did not know the word "coot," and because the hard C and G, and T and D look alike on the lips he read the sentence as "He's good," and took this to refer to his playing. They thought he was a good football player, so he was prepared now to be generous. He picked up the ball and climbed to his feet.

"Eyarr," he said, meaning: "Here you are," and tossed the ball towards his captain almost with smugness.

At any other time the boys would have acknowledged that David did not realize what had happened; but in their present mood his cheery flippancy and self-satisfied gesture aggravated them all the more.

"He wants to play!" one of them jeered.

He can't hear. He can't hear. He makes noises like an ani-

mal. The creepiness was frightening. Fear, mistrust, and ignorance combined to arouse the mob instinct in them, and
they drew closer together. From the background Ted was
watching his opportunity.

"You're not going to let him get away with it, are you?" and
again Ted's insidious voice urged them into action.

The ball lay untouched where David had thrown it, and
gazing at the hostile faces he at last knew their anger was di-
rected towards himself. Amazed and bewildered he backed a
step. The lips before him clamped shut. The eyes narrowed at
him. On one face the teeth were white behind a mouth that
leered at him. The tip of another boy's tongue came out to roll
its way round his lips.

Someone behind the crowd pushed forward, and the boys
shuffled forward as a body. David backed another step, turned,
and ran.

This was the signal for the full-blooded chase. With yells
and whoops the boys released their pent-up fear in the only
way they knew.

David's way home was blocked by Ted, whose bulk and
threatening manner together were more than he felt willing to
chance. Without the slightest idea of why the boys had so sur-
prisingly turned on him, David swerved into the Guests' garden, meaning to approach his own home from the back. By the
time he had climbed the fence he saw that a stream of boys
were pouring up his own garden as well as the adjacent ones.

"Why? Why?" he asked himself.

His only line of retreat was up the Bank, and he tugged at
the mallow bushes and long damp grass to pull himself up the
steep path.

"Why?"

His foot slipped on some loose gravel as he glanced back-
ward to see what was happening. Boys were climbing over the

garden fences and those in front were already approaching the
Bank. He thought he saw Eileen waving from the garden, but
he did not know to whom and did not stop to consider. Already
gasping for breath he dug his toes in the gravel and climbed
up farther.

"Stop!" Eileen was yelling. "Stop! You can't do that to him!"
Her appeal was ignored, except by Tommy, who hesitated.
Eileen grabbed him and asked what was happening.

"He—he—cheated at football, and——"

"The idiots!" was her comment. "Don't they understand he
can't hear and probably doesn't even know what's wrong?
Wait here, and I'll stop them."

Eileen followed the crowd, who were now deploying round
the Bank and beginning to climb it from all three sides: the
fourth side merged into the hill which rose above it. David
had reached the top and she could see him standing there,
watching what was happening, and no doubt gathering breath
and strength for the next move.

"Stop!" cried Eileen. "Wait for me, and I'll explain." But
her voice was lost with the wind and the general panting
scrabble through the grass and scrub.

David saw the heads, hands, and legs bobbing and clawing
up towards him from three sides. One boy looked up at him
and appeared to say something, but it was a face he had not
seen before. He saw Eileen running to catch up with everyone
else, her arms still waving, and she, too, appeared to be saying
something.

"Eileen? Why Eileen?" But he had no time to speculate. He
glanced behind him at the path which ran along the level
summit of the Bank to join others on the hillside. There was
no cover and his pursuers were now more than halfway up the
Bank. He waited a few moments more. Then, picking a gap
between two boys who were farther apart than most, he

plunged down the steep grassy slope, to leap and lurch between them, crying aloud as he went. Taken by surprise they
made no effort to catch him, but the unknown boy tore a clod
of grass and earth which he flung after David, now making off
along the hillside towards a hedge. The violent action had the
effect of rallying all those in sight, and with more yells and
whoops they plunged after him. Some half-dozen boys who
were climbing the far side of the Bank reached the top to find
their quarry gone and themselves too far behind to catch up
with the main body of hunters. They cheered the others on
and sat down to rest and watch the outcome.

"Hide. Hide," David told himself.

He reached the hedge of stunted trees and thorn bushes,
and pushed his way through. For a moment he crouched down
and looked back, to see three of his former teammates not far
off and a bunch of more boys some way behind. He looked
around to work out his next move. Downwards the hedge
thinned out above the gardens of that end of the estate: upwards and at right angles was another hedge that he recognized.

"Field—horses—eat."

Crouching low to use the cover, he made his way up the
hillside to the next hedge, crawled up the banked earth, and
dropped behind a tree. Here he peered down to see if his pursuers were still after him.

Three boys had seen him and were jogging upwards. He
ducked down, and, half crawling, half running, dodged from
tree to bush and tree along the edge of the field. Halfway
across was a holly bush which should give him ample cover if
he could reach it in time. Not daring to look behind him and
not realizing that his unconscious grunts and panting were
loud enough to be heard from some distance, he at last reached
his next refuge. He flung himself full length in the long grass

beneath an overhanging bough thickly leafed. Fortunately, the wind had carried his cries uphill and away from the other boys.

Having to rely on his eyesight for all knowledge of what was happening, he peered back along the way he had come. He saw that though the three boys had come through the second and higher hedge, they now seemed to have lost track of him and were scanning the hill in all directions. David dropped back into the grass, but he presently had another peep, to watch them crawling back through the hedge having apparently given up the chase. Or were they following him on the far side? He allowed himself a few minutes rest to get back his breath, and lay with his head on one arm.

The two dray horses that were usually put out to grass over the weekend were standing at the far end of the field near the gate at the top. When he had come this way once with Michael, they had let him stroke their noses, and he remembered the soft, friendly, and inquiring nuzzle the gray one had given his hand. Thinking of Michael made him want to ask Michael why all this was happening.

He lay in the grass, which was wet and cool against his cheeks and hands, and felt calmer. He ceased to pant; but he kept a watch along the hedge and the far side of the field. A movement near the gate caught his eye and he propped himself on his elbows to see more clearly.

The stranger, walking his bicycle, passed the gate and continued along the cart-track. David lay back again. The grass felt chilly now and he could feel the dampness seeping through his clothes, so he cautiously squatted on his heels and peeped through the leaves. No one was in sight below, and he made his way back to the corner of the field where the hedge lying up the hill joined the one he was hiding behind.

Still on the watch for lurking pursuers, he dropped down

the bank into the field below, and walked slowly downwards, keeping under cover of the hedge.

He intended to reach the top gardens of the estate and then make his way home as best he could. But before he had crossed half the width of the field he was taken by surprise, when three boys burst through the hedge ahead of him.

David broke into a run, and swerved across the open field. From the corner of his eye he caught a glimpse of more boys lurching at him from above, their mouths open, their hands outstretched. He changed course, and ran for the gate at the lower far corner.

He stumbled over the uneven ground and tufts of grass in his effort to escape from faces peering and mouths flapping at him. Mouths everywhere, pouting, stretching, shutting, flapping. Red panting faces, and hands that clawed at him.

He lifted his arms in an attempt to push the visions away, and fled on.

8

✳ *The tunnel*

"Dark—hide. Dark—hide," said David to himself.

The entrance to the canal tunnel opened ahead of him, though he had not deliberately sought it. Its secret blackness was inviting, and the darkness offered relief from the faces and mouths. There would be no one to bully, hunt, or talk at him.

He ran past an empty coal barge standing high in the water, and as he went farther into the cutting, the banked hillside shut out more and more of the world on either side.

"Run—hide—dark."

The towpath curved inwards as the canal narrowed. He was between high blackened brick walls which screened the sun and cast a deepening shadow over the already murky water. The entrance to the tunnel itself was rounded and built on the same lines as a railway tunnel, the only difference being that the towpath continued along its whole length, like a long Tube station platform. The path had been built wide enough

to allow two barge horses to pass each other. On the brick facing of the arch was a notice forbidding entry to any unauthorized person.

"Dark—dark—dark."

The twilight coolness of the first hundred yards was sooth-
ing, and David pressed on to find the blackness which would
blot out the visions and memories.

The towpath was built of brick, and at about two-foot intervals a row of bricks was raised about an inch across the path to
form a series of ridges. This had been done to prevent the
horses slipping as they dragged the laden barges. David stumbled over the ridges for a while, until he learned automatically
to adjust the length of his stride.

As his eyes became used to the intensifying darkness, he
saw the round disc of light ahead which was the daylight at
the far end. It was impossible to judge how far away the other
end was. The hole might have been the size of a mousehole at
the end of a room, or a colossal cave entrance at the foot of a
vast mountain miles across.

"No people. Dark good."

With his right hand he kept contact with the wall, so as not
to walk too near the edge, for presently it was impossible to see
either the path or the water. Also he wanted to find a recess or
some spot where he could lie down and curl up.

Losing sense of time and distance, he walked on as if in a
dream; his feet on the path sometimes stubbing a toe or catching a heel on one of the brick edges; his hand touching the
brick wall lightly and swinging for the next contact. With
nothing else on which to focus his eyes, he watched the daylight ahead steadily, until out of the darkness it became distorted and appeared to jump about. He blinked, but the round
light patch grew more and more like a face.

He shut his eyes to blot out the vision and walked on, and

where the face had been was now a dense black shape sur-
rounded by a gray halo which moved up and down under his
eyelids in time to his footsteps, but it was more like a bouncing
football than a face. It swam about for a while and slowly
faded away, so he walked on with closed eyes. It was easier to
keep walking in a steady rhythm than to stop and think.

For a long time he walked in an irregular rhythm, three-
long-steps-one-short-one, and tried to think of nothing. The
harder he tried to wipe out his thoughts, the more persistent
they became, so he counted his footsteps: one hundred, two
hundred, three—or was it four hundred? He stopped count-
ing, to wonder if he had reached the other end of the tunnel
yet; and he opened his eyes to find that the far end was almost
as far away as before. The white circle of daylight was larger
and more like a face which moved in time to his footsteps, a
round white blank face, that looked at him with hostility.

"Bad-boys-Mich-ael-bad-boys-Mich-ael——" Even the words
fitted the rhythm. He shut his eyes again, and continued walking.

When he next opened his eyes, the disc of daylight ahead
appeared to be only slightly nearer. As his vision adjusted itself, he was surprised to find that he could see the edge of the
path outlined against the water, and some way ahead was a
pale silvery streak across the water. In the middle of the tunnel and out of darkness, light was coming from somewhere.
He walked toward the soft moonlight effect. It was farther
away than he had thought. At last, as he drew nearer, the tunnel became distinctly lighter, until he was able to see what
appeared to be a hole in the roof through which the daylight
was entering.

David stood beneath a circular brick hole and peered upwards. This was no way out; but an air vent, cut like a chimney and bricked up like a well. There was a circle of sky at the

top, which was perhaps fifty, perhaps a hundred and fifty feet away.

Suddenly David felt small, lost, and far from home, and he shivered in the slight draught.

It may have been a cloud which drifted across the opening, or it may have been his tired senses which distorted and exaggerated all he saw. As he gazed upwards the friendly blueness changed to white, and gray shadows moved like lips.

"More faces. Home. Home."

Wildly he turned round to look backwards, and saw that the entrance where he had come in was now another face, the same size as the one he had been looking at all the way. He was halfway through the canal tunnel.

He looked down at the water, and a sodden gray sheet of torn newspaper looked up at him: in the gentlest motion of the water, it moved. The face of another footballer watched him accusingly.

He flung up his arms to hide his eyes, turned, and began to run home. He tripped over a brick, and having lost his guiding contact with the wall, he tottered, tripped over another brick, and plunged into the water. In the confined space his shriek reverberated the whole length of the tunnel, more than half a mile in each direction.

David was not normally afraid of water and was a good swimmer. Having fallen in with his mouth open, he came to the surface spitting out the foul taste of soot, coal dust, oil, and other indefinable flavors. He twisted and splurted, and struck out for the path. He climbed out with some difficulty, and lay full length, panting and spitting.

He probably fainted. Coughing up water, he realized he must have been lying there a long while. A row of bricks was pressing painfully into his ribs, another across his knees, and there was grit in his mouth. Above all he was cold. A shiver would start somewhere between his shoulder blades to spread in ripples over his body and down the backs of his legs, almost flapping his wet clothes as it gripped his skin and muscles. Before one ripple had reached his feet, the next was already spreading down his back.

"Mother, mother, mother, mother."

For some time he lay there longing to be home yet not daring to look at the terrifying length of tunnel that lay between him and the world outside. A more violent shiver hurt his knees so much that he shifted his position. He made himself stand up. He rolled his tongue round his mouth to collect as many bits of grit as he could, and spat them out, but the taste of soot and oil remained. Then he started on his long way home, his hand as before swinging to keep contact with the wall.

There were no visions now, no faces or footballs. Nothing except his wet clothes, the path, the wall, the blackness, and, many many miles away, home.

The circle of daylight ahead of him did not seem to come any nearer, indeed it appeared to move farther away. He turned to look behind at the opposite end to reassure himself that that one at least was becoming smaller and more distant.

He grew to hate the brick ridges. Every fourth one interrupted the natural length of his stride, so every alternate step he made with his left foot had to be shortened, or lengthened, or uncomfortably placed on the narrow brick. He tried altering his step so that the right foot would take the awkward rhythm, but he kicked his big toe where he had already kicked it once before He wanted shoes or boots to kick the beastly bricks, instead of soggy sandals.

He began to work himself into a temper, though there was nothing on which he could release it without hurting himself all the more. So he went on walking and hating.

"Bad bricks. Bad tunnel. Bad, bad, bad."

It seemed very much farther going back than it had coming in. It was only after apparent hours of walking that almost imperceptibly the tunnel entrance began to lose its round shape: the level of the water flattened the bottom, and the shape of the raised path appeared in silhouette. The water lost its dense blackness to become dark gray.

He began to see the shapes beyond the blank dazzle of light that had been his view since he came in, and noticed that the coal barge which had been lying at the entrance for the past week had gone. Because of a slight bend in the canal, he could not see beyond the high brick walls that banked up the cutting in the hill. He stepped out of the tunnel and on to the plain cinder towpath with an enormous sense of relief. Only as he rounded the bend into the direct sunlight did he notice anything strange.

Not a hundred yards away, where there should have been rough grass and reeds bordering the water, a great black iron bridge crossed the canal, and, as he watched, a red double-decker bus moved over it.

David stood and gaped. There should be no big bridge here. His home should be round the corner on the right, and the road into Bitter End should run below the level of the canal, only crossing it farther on. He looked for the little brick foot-bridge, but it was not there. He ran on to get a wider view, and a whole strange landscape of factory buildings and blank black walls was all he could see. He sat down where he was on the cinders, trying to push the truth from him—only his brain kept repeating:

"Wrong way—tunnel end not front. Wrong way."

He put his head on his knees and allowed his aching feet and leg muscles a rest. Presently a new sensation crept over his back, the warmth of the sun. He felt it penetrating his wet

shirt. He felt his tense muscles slacken, and, as he relaxed, his natural buoyancy revived. He clasped his hands round his ankles for comfort, and found that his right hand was sore. Holding it up he saw that it was black, and scratched, and the nails were torn.

"Right hand dirty. Left hand good clean. Right hand touch tunnel—not left hand. All the way? Turn back left hand touch tunnel."

Coming straight through the tunnel, his right hand had always been on the wall; had he turned back, his left hand would have guided him. His numbed and semi-conscious state after falling in the water had left him without any sense of direction or ability to think. He had gone on with his right hand on the wall.

"Silly fool David. Michael laugh. Michael? Michael football. Football—boys—run—faces—faces——"

It all came flooding back and he climbed to his feet.

The only way home that he knew was through the tunnel. But nothing would have persuaded him to go back that way. "No."

Home was over the hill, and if he walked straight up, across, and down towards the sunset, he could hardly avoid hitting the road somewhere between Bitter End and Blackley.

Walking to the bridge, he found steps up to the road, but climbing these proved to be of little help. A glance in both directions showed him factory walls, buildings, sheds, houses, gates, and small shops with no apparent way through to the top. Turning left because the road seemed to climb slightly across the slope. David set out to find a way home.

He turned up a couple of alleys, to find them blocked by tall wooden gates which were locked. He walked up a road lined with terraced houses on either side, only to round two corners and find himself going down to the main road again.

"No road."

A bus came toward him; but he did not recognize any of the names displayed on its route board.

"No bus."

Nevertheless he felt in his damp pockets and brought out a couple of sixpenny bits and a few coppers—which made him think of food. A bend in the road took him downhill towards some shops, and, hoping to find a baker's or sweet shop, he wandered on. Passing a large building, he noticed what looked like a carved and decorated tombstone set in the wall, slender pillars supporting a canopy under which was a tablet bearing an inscription. A tap and a metal cup attached to a chain caught his eye.

"Water."

He rinsed his mouth, slaked his thirst, and washed his hands and face at the elaborate Victorian drinking fountain. Then he went on to a small general store, where he bought a bar of chocolate. Standing on the pavement corner to eat it, he considered his next move. He had always been told that if he were lost or in trouble, he must find a policeman. With this in mind he turned into another street full of people, shops, and traffic. He dreaded trying to make himself understood to any stranger in the street, but a policeman would be different. Policemen were clever. They could do so many things that they might be able to finger-spell.

He walked the whole length of the shopping area without so much as seeing a blue helmet, and at the next main road junction he stopped to consider his position again. Of the three roads before him, one was a narrow lane which was not promising; one ran straight across to a residential area; and the third on his left went downhill across open marshland, past a railway yard, and joined what looked like a major trunk road with a stream of traffic.

He decided hopefully to go on down to the busier road. From this height he could see it bending out of sight in what he thought was roughly the direction of Blackley.

The first road was longer than it had looked. Before he reached the railway yard, he turned to glance back the way he had come. He saw that he was walking farther and farther away from the hills—the range of hills he knew must be Windbell Edge.

As he looked at the clustering town below the Edge he began to doubt that he had walked through its streets. He began to doubt that he had walked through the tunnel under the hill. Not a thing here did he know or recognize: he had walked through darkness to an unknown land where he was alone, entirely and completely alone.

"Mother!" his spirit cried to the hills, and without knowing it his voice echoed his cry. He longed for his own close, loving family, the familiar shape of Llandudno and the Welsh hills, for the familiar corridors and classrooms at school, for something or someone he knew; but the cars passed him by like giant beetles, unseeing and uncaring.

Doubtfully he glanced at the junction ahead, and watched a red double-decker bus pass across. Buses were the only things in the whole of his present world that he knew and understood and that could help him. David walked on wearily.

He made for a bus shelter, but before he had time to study the timetables a bus drew up. Among several other names displayed on its route, he read Blackley. Thankfully he climbed aboard.

When the ticket-man came for his fare, he held out his remaining change. Twice he tried to say Blackley, but he was too tired to concentrate on flicking his tongue round the difficult "ckly" sound and the ticket-man did not understand. Patiently David sketched the letters with a finger on the empty seat beside him. With a kindly smile the man shook his head and pointed to the back of the bus.

David tried again. The man searched his pocket for a pencil and paper, scribbled something which David read as Birmingham, and pointed in the direction in which they were travelling. Blackley, he indicated, was behind them. When David understood he was travelling away from home, not towards it, tears stung around the edges of his eyes.

At the next stop, the ticket-man took the trouble to keep his own bus waiting while he saw David safely across the traffic to the bus shelter on the opposite side of the road. He wrote down the number of the bus he needed. David felt the friendly squeeze on his shoulder, and he smiled his thanks.

Installed at last on the right bus, all David's worries left him. The ticket-man had taken his last sixpence and two of the four coppers, so he knew the journey would be fairly long. There were few people on the top deck, and after the long afternoon's sun it was warm and stuffy. He took off his sandals to inspect the blisters on his heels, and the relief of taking his feet out of the still soggy shoes was so great he did not put them back on. For comfort he tucked his feet under him. Presently he would have to watch for landmarks so that he would know when to get off, but he allowed himself a few minutes rest, and curled up on the seat. The sun shone to warm his back and the motion of the bus dulled his senses. He closed his eyes and thought of the tea that would be waiting for him at home.

The ticket-man looked cross when he woke him. Still half asleep, David fumbled for his sandals and clopped awkwardly down the stairs. The ticket-man was trying to tell him something. He had him by the arm and was earnestly talking to him, but David made no attempt to lip-read. He was too tired to make the effort. The easiest thing to do was to nod as though he had understood, and be gone. When the bus stopped, he pushed past the people waiting to get on, and stooped on the pavement to do up his sandals. Then he stood up to make his way home.

This was not any part of Blackley that he knew. The bus had left him at a large roundabout where some five or six roads met. He looked further afield for some familiar landmark. There was a hill covered with trees behind a cluster of factory buildings, but it bore no resemblance to Windbell Edge, nor could he find any building, church spire, or chimney which could give him any indication of where he was. There was nothing to tell him he was in Blackley. It might have been any town anywhere.

"How long sleep? What say ticket-man?" He could no longer keep the questions from his mind, nor could he help admitting that he was more lost than before. Had he slept all the way through Blackley? How far away was home? And where? Previously he had known that home lay over the hills, but here there was nothing that he knew.

Desperation drove him to seek help from hearing people. He crossed to a garage on the next corner. He waited while the man dealt with a customer. Then, making a determined effort to articulate each sound clearly, David approached him and said:

"I ahm losst. Belackerlee."

The man looked surprised and David saw him say "What?" He repeated his words, not realizing that they were drowned as a motorcycle came in for petrol. The garageman made a vague movement with his hands that might have been an invitation to wait. David waited while two more cars came in. The motorcycle and first car were served with petrol; the second car wanted air in its tires as well.

David saw a woman pushing a pram on the other side of the road, so he left the garage, dodged the traffic, and ran to catch her up. Two other young children were walking by the pram and one was pushing a cart. David touched her arm to attract attention.

"I ahm losst. Belackerlee."

He watched her expression change from astonishment to sympathetic enquiry. He repeated his words, together with the finger-spelling, to make sure she understood he was deaf, and he saw a smile of sympathy on her face. She spoke to him, and he watched her lips carefully.

"What have you lost?" He saw the first and last words, and nodded vigorously. She had understood.

"Belackerlee. 'Ome."

"What?"

If he had a pencil and paper with him, he could simply have written down his address, but if he could not make her understand Blackley, would she ever hear Windbell Edge? The noise of the traffic made it all the more difficult for her to hear him, let alone understand what he was saying. Patiently he drew in the air the outline of the letters, B-L-A-.

The child with the cart had walked ahead and was dangerously near the edge of the pavement. The woman pushed the pram after him and pulled him back on to the footpath. Now the little girl was talking to her and pulling at her skirt. David waited impatiently until she could give him her attention; then he tried again, B-L-A-C-K. She was talking to him. He saw her lips moving, too fast for him to follow, and shook his head. She spoke again, exaggerating her lip movements into grimaces unrecognizable as words. Neither of them knew what the other was trying to say.

With a sad but not unkind smile the woman shook her head and walked on, the children scampering with her. David could not know that she thought he had lost something black, and not that he himself was lost. As she had not seen anything that might be his, she did not think that she could be of any help.

He must find someone with a pen or pencil. He looked back at the garage, and there were now three cars waiting for petrol. He looked round for a shop, and across the road saw the back of a large traffic signpost. That could tell him in which direction Blackley lay.

The traffic made his head whirl as again he crossed the road at the roundabout. He had forgotten now which road he had started from, or from what direction the bus had brought him. Cars, buses, lorries, vans, motorcycles rushed at him from first one side and then the other, and when he reached the huge sheet of metal that bore the names and numbers of the roads, he had to steady himself before he could look up to read it. He saw the plan of the roundabout with roads branching off, each to a different place name, only Blackley was not among them. He screwed his eyes shut and looked again, reading the names slowly round from the bottom left over to the bottom right, five different roads leading to five different places, and Blackley was nowhere.

David sat on the narrow grass verge, put his hands on his knees and gave up. Darkness enveloped him, and out of the darkness the faces came back to haunt him, floating before his eyes, circling the roundabouts; eyes blinking at him; mouths talking at him, lips twisting, grinning, snapping at him. He looked up to make them go away and found himself staring stupidly at a telephone box a few feet away. A man came out and spoke to him, for he seemed to think that David was waiting to make a call. David shook his head dully, and the man walked away. David knew that hearing people could talk to each other along the telephone wires, and could use them to call for help when they needed it. They could talk to their

friends, summon a doctor, do business, and a hundred other things; but the telephone was of no use to him.

Suddenly he was swept by a wave of terror and desolation. People everywhere who could help him so easily if they were able to; ordinary homely people who looked kind until the moment they realized he was deaf, and then they would become frightened by their own ignorance of how to talk to him. People who could hear, who were clever, who could talk to the telephone, but who could not tell him how to get home, whom he could not tell he was lost.

Terror swept him to his feet in a wild, blind panic; a moving, seething, horrifying sequence of visions crowded over him; traffic sweeping past always, vibrating, smelly monsters that threatened to crush him, slipping across the corner of his eyes and making him reel towards them with compulsive dizziness; red buses bearing down on him, deceiving him again and again with their blank, staring windows; faces looking at him, staring faces, blank open mouths, round and dark as footballs; mouths opening, flapping, snapping; teeth grinning at him, white teeth coming and going. People running after. People running; arms clawing at him; hands grabbing, mouths open, faces all around. Michael's face mocking him in the disttance. Michael—football—run. Dark good. Dark hide. Run—dark—hide. Michael's face coming closer, mouths open, moving, flapping, stretching. Hands grabbing, clutching at him.

Michael's face coming, going, coming. Michael's hands, arms, jacket. Michael's face, real alive. Michael's hands, arms, the curl on his forehead.

Michael to take him home. He clutched at him with both hands, a solid, living body whom he knew, who could talk to him, who could understand him. David clung to him with trembling hands.

9

* *Michael takes over*

After the enjoyment of watching the Wolves win their match, Michael had gone to a friend's home near Wolverhampton for tea.

In the bus, on the way back to Blackley, he gazed out of the window without taking in the passing scene. He looked straight at David as the bus swerved through the roundabout; but it was not until the bus was past that something made Michael crane his head round to look again. He caught only a brief glimpse of the red head and the dirty, striped green and white shirt that looked familiar. It was the appealing, outstretched arms that decided him, the wild, desperate fling of the body.

Without considering further, Michael scrambled down the steps and got off at the next stop. He began to run back the two hundred yards to the roundabout. Now he was cursing himself as a silly sentimental fool. He must have been mistaken in the bus, for there was no reason why David should be running there alone, looking as if he had come out of a coal-pit, and miles from home. It was sure to be some scruffy youth well able to look after himself and who would hoot with laughter if he knew that Michael was coming to his help on an impulse. But, having abandoned the bus, he might as well satisfy his curiosity now that he was here. Though he slackened his pace, he looked closely at the boy coming towards him.

For weeks afterwards Michael was to remember the look in David's eyes as disbelief gave way to recognition.

David clung to Michael for the first few minutes like the proverbial drowning man clinging to a straw. He attempted to voice his troubles, but the desperation of his combination of speech, finger-spelling, signs, and miming gave Michael little idea as to what was the matter.

To some extent Michael had learned to recognize David's speech, and he could often guess what David was trying to say. Sometimes he could feel his own throat constrained and working in sympathy with the effort David made to formulate words he had never heard; and at the best of times David needed all the concentration and skill he was able to command in order to say the simplest of sentences. Tired and confused as he was at the moment, he lost nearly all control over his voice, and resorted to fast and elaborate gestures which told Michael little. He was using every means he knew to express his relief and gratitude, his anxiety, and his long story all at once.

Hearing people find themselves at a loss for words on some occasions when they are shocked, pleased or distressed, or words come bubbling over with excitement in a way that is often incoherent. David had no way of expressing himself that was not laborious, clumsy, slow, and almost always inadequate. He had not the language at his command: he simply did not know enough words to cover all he wanted to say.

He did not know why he had been hunted, or why he had

seen faces. He could not tell Michael the facts of what had happened, let alone why they had happened.

Michael's first thought was that perhaps David's family had had some accident; and his second that David had become involved with a gang of burglars, and had been roughly handled. This led to wilder guesses: perhaps he had been kidnapped, or the house burnt down. He must find out what had happened, and he did his best to calm David down. Presently he heard two words that David repeated over and over again: " 'Ome. Losst."

"W-H-Y?" he finger-spelled.

This was followed by a series of gestures which seemed to imply first that David was running, then that he was swimming, and lastly with that universal gesture of folding the hands against a cheek and closing the eyes that he had been sleeping.

"W-H-Y-R-U-N?" Michael finger-spelled slowly, taking him back to the beginning.

Seeing that he was at last beginning to make himself understood, David took more control of himself. Neither of them had a pencil, so with a deep breath he began to sketch out the words, letter by letter with a finger on the pavement where they were sitting. Though he could have finger-spelled it more quickly, Michael followed him more easily that way.

"B-O-Y-S-R-U-N-A-F-T-E-R," and pointed to himself.

"W-H-Y?" Michael asked, and David shrugged his shoulders to dismiss a question that was beyond his comprehension.

David continued his story by pointing to himself and then spelling out: "T-U-N-N-E-L."

"What?"

David mimed the action of running, and spelled the word out again.

"T-R-A-I-N?" Michael asked.

"W-A-T-E-R."

"Oh, I see, the canal tunnel. Why?"

Without the necessity of lip-reading David saw the comprehension on Michael's face. He followed on by miming the action of diving to indicate he had fallen in. This was confusing to Michael, and David's next word was all the more confusing, for he simply spelled out:

"F-A-C-E-S," and looked wildly from side to side to show his fear. Assuming that Michael was following his explanation he mimed his running action again, and wrote:

"R-O-N-G-E-N-D-L-O-S-T," which Michael read as "rongend lost." For a moment he wondered what was meant by a "rongend" and where it had been lost, until he separated the letters and mentally corrected the spelling, all of which caused him to lose track of what David was now writing. He saw David wipe out the shadow of some words before he continued:

"B-U-S," and pointed to the spot on which they were sitting. "Losst. 'Ome please."

Michael had given up trying to understand. If David had not obviously been serious in his account, he would have scoffed at the whole thing as a leg-pull or a bad nightmare. Perhaps David had been frightened by a horror film. He looked again at David, his hair streaked with mud, his face smeared, his shirt greasy and black.

"Lost. 'Ome please," repeated David, and with movements of his hands to his mouth demonstrated that he was hungry and thirsty. Michael gave up all attempts to find out more. He sprang to action and pulled David to his feet. In doing so he felt the wet belt round his shorts and knew that somewhere somehow David had been in water.

He led David to the bus stop farther up the road. David was already on the Blackley road, and that was the reason why the name had not appeared on the signpost, which was intended for traffic leaving the town. By now it was past seven o'clock: the evening traffic was thin, and the buses less frequent. They waited ten minutes. David began to shiver in waves and spasms that jerked his body, and Michael gave him his own jacket to put on. He could see that David was exhausted, by his strained face and by the way he flopped against the wall of the bus shelter. Still there was no bus.

Michael saw a taxi swing round the bend towards them and boldly stepped out to call it. The driver stopped but when he saw that two boys were to be his fares, he began to look suspicious.

"Where d'you want to go?"

"The other side of Blackley."

"Cost you over seven shillings. Have you got it?"

"No. But my father will pay."

"What d'you take me for? I'm not carrying kids around for nothing."

"We're going home and Dad will pay, really."

"Nothing doing, son," and he turned back into his driving seat.

"Look, my friend's ill. He's fallen in some water and I'm afraid he may get pneumonia."

"Where? There's no water to fall in round here."

"I don't know. I just found him."

"You don't say. Think of something better next time."

"But he did," and he pulled David forward.

"Well, sonny, you look a mess which is all the more reason why I'm not taking you in my cab."

"He can't hear you. He's deaf and dumb. Please take us."

The driver looked at David more closely.

"How do I know he's deaf and dumb? That's the easiest thing to put on."

"I can't prove it, but he is."

"What's wrong with the bus?"

"We've waited for ages, and he's shivering terribly badly. Please."

"What happened?"

"I don't know. I think it's too complicated for him to explain."

"All right. Hop in. But if you lead me a dance you're in for trouble, and no mistake."

Michael pushed David in, climbed after him, and hoped that either his mother or father would be at home when they arrived. They would certainly make a fuss about all that money, but he couldn't help it. He couldn't have stood watching David any longer. David dropped thankfully into the seat, and in no time it seemed they were through Blackley and on the road out to the estate. Michael started to give directions.

"It's the next road on the left, then you take the first bend round on the right, and we're at the top."

"Well, I don't know about trouble," said the driver as he swung round the bend, "but you look as though you've got a packet coming to you. Police car and all."

Michael peered up the hill, and saw the car outside David's house, where a crowd of curious children hung about.

10

* *The return*

The Williamses were sitting down to their meal before David was missed. They gave him a few minutes grace and finished the salad. It was no good trying to call him, and they had to trust his sense of time and hunger to get him to meals punctually.

It was not until they had finished the apple tart and cream and had drunk their cups of tea, that Eric volunteered to have a look for him.

The obvious place to start was at the Guests', where Eileen gave him a brief account of the hunt she had tried to stop. By seven-thirty Eric, Eileen, and Mr. Williams had searched the surrounding hillside. Tommy had gathered some of the boys who had been in the football game, and they searched by the canal, the railway yard, and the roads around Bitter End. They reported their failure unwillingly for they were by no means confident they were not going to be blamed for David's

absence; but no comment was made either by his parents or by Eric. Mr. Williams was reluctant to call the police, and it was only when two girls had reported hearing a scream from the tunnel that he finally agreed.

The police car arrived a few minutes before the taxi.

Michael climbed out of the taxi after David, told the driver he would be back with the money soon, and followed David into his home prepared to battle on his behalf.

"I found him on the road near Wolverhampton," Michael announced to the room at large, for it seemed to contain a crowd of people. He wondered why Eileen and Tommy were there.

"Wolverhampton! But how——"

"I don't know."

"But that's miles away!"

"He was in an awful panic."

"Do you know what happened?"

"Can you give me some money for——"

David, having come from his mother's hug, broke into his own animated version of the story. Then he saw the crowd of people in the room: a row of faces watching him, one of them a policeman. Were they curious, accusing, or threatening? He was in no condition to cope with more people, more faces, or lip-reading, and he shrank back.

Later that evening Michael and Eileen went back to hear David's story. Having luxuriated in a hot bath and eaten a good supper, David was anxious to tell as much as he could.

In many ways and because he had grown up with him, Eric was closer to his brother than either of their parents. He now brought the story out from David and interpreted it to everyone else. With a quick and versatile mixture of finger-spelling, signs, speech, lip-reading, miming, and paper and pencil, Eric took David back to the game of football, where the story appeared to have started.

Michael leaned forward from his corner fascinated by Eric's ability to converse by these means: the momentary flick of a finger or hand that seemed to ask a whole question; the patient breaking down of David's impulsive answers to get more details; David's animated facial, hand, and body movements that a professional actor might have envied, and the finger-gymnastics that were as quick and supple as a violinist's. Michael suddenly knew how clumsy and amateurish were his own attempts to converse with David. He began to doubt if he would ever break through such a barrier of silence with almost no language.

"He says that he ran away to hide in the tunnel. He saw faces back and front—I don't know what he means by that. He fell in."

"So he was in the tunnel!" exclaimed Michael.

"He was very frightened, and came out at the wrong end."

"But it's a mile and a half long," was Michael's comment. "No wonder he looked done up. Gee whizz, none of us has ever done that before!"

"He says he was lost, so he found a bus."

"Where?"

"On a big road. He'll mean a main road."

"That must be the main Birmingham road. That's a good couple of miles or so from the tunnel."

"He seems to have got on a wrong bus somehow. He went to sleep, and when he got off he was more lost, and more frightened. Then Michael came."

The following morning small groups of boys shuffled about the estate and along the towpath.

"But why didn't you tell us he's deaf and dumb?"

"I should have thought everyone knew that."

"I've never seen the kid before. We don't know everyone up your end."

"We thought it was an ordinary rag, or we wouldn't have pounced on him like that at the end."

"But why were you ragging him anyway? He didn't start it."

"He got us ratty. Oh, and it was queer—sort of creepy—him not being able to hear a word we said, and making noises."

"And there was Ted."

"How does Ted come into it?"

"I don't know. He was egging us on."

"Haven't you heard?" asked an older boy who had been the captain of David's team. "Ted's girl friend has been making eyes at Eric, David's brother. He wanted to get his own back, I expect."

"Well, of all the nasty tricks! But that was no reason for you to hunt him down either."

"Here, don't put all the blame on us."

"I'm not."

"The point is, what do we do now?"

"I don't know."

Elsewhere Paul was telling Tommy:

"I still think David was mean in his playing."

"Eileen said he can't help being like that."

"I think he's mad."

"Well, you'd better keep out of Michael's way then, because Michael's mad with all of us. And it was you who knocked him down."

"Ted told me to."

"And you got a scooter ride for that."

"Aw, shut up, can't you?"

Eileen and Michael were cleaning their shoes together.

"Don't take on so," said Eileen. "It wasn't your fault."

"I know. But I can't think what possessed them to hunt him like that. I—I could knock their heads together—and worse."

"Why not just let it simmer down? After all Eric will straighten it all out for David."

"Mmm."

"Eric's not silly about David. He's very fond of him, and sensible at the same time. Not like those people who put on a special expression and start to fuss, as soon as they see someone disabled or something."

"I should hope not."

"And he's nice as well. Oh, I forgot to tell you. Tommy says that the police gave Ted a ticking off last night. That should take him down a peg or two."

"Well, that's the best news yet."

David himself was given breakfast in bed that morning. He wallowed in the unaccustomed luxury, and decided to mark it by eating the toast and marmalade first and finishing off with the boiled egg. He was slightly stiff but otherwise none the worse for his experiences of the previous day; he was content to sit downstairs later and carry on with his models.

Michael came to see him during the morning, and was relieved to find him so cheerful. He gave David a small collection of matches to add to the store.

II

✳ *Boatbuilders*

During the days that followed David started the matchstick castle, for the time being leaving the shops and houses, and the school that was only half built.

He had drawn a square castle-plan, and because it was more interesting he began with the round towers at each of the corners. For these he first cut a circular groove in the wood to form the foundation, and then fitted the matches upright in it, gluing each match to the next like a palisade, and cutting alternate matches slightly shorter to give a crenellated effect.

While his father was away driving the lorry all night and Eric at his evening classes, David sat happily at the table; his mother sewed or did various jobs about the house. The first tower was built within a week, and, pleased with the result, David completed the second over a weekend.

Meanwhile Michael returned to his old friends. Three of them were carrying out their plan of building a raft, which they hoped to launch on the canal. They had found a couple of old railway sleepers, across which they began nailing planks. Their numbers grew, and they decided to dismantle the original raft, half completed, in order to make two. Making a crude keel of each sleeper, they intended to nail the planks along its length.

With his friends' agreement, Michael asked David if he would like to join them.

"Will you make a boat with us?" was how Michael put it, for he was learning David's limitations of language.

"Yes," was the ready reply. David himself had had to extract permission to join the football game which had ended so disastrously: now, a real invitation, and from Michael, was different; Michael was not only his first hearing friend but also his interpreter and guide among the other hearing boys. Without him David might well have been in China or Afghanistan, for all he could understand of what was being said.

When David arrived at the towpath, he was dismayed to find that two of the boys had been among those who had hunted him across the slopes of Windbell Edge. One of them had been the captain of the team for which he had played. They greeted him with smiles, and he smiled back a little apprehensively, for he did not know if they were to be friends or not. He turned to Michael for guidance, but Michael was unaware of his difficulty, and introduced them easily. David learnt that his former captain's name was Dick and that the other boy was called Peter.

Then Michael set him to work with a pair of pincers, drawing out the nails from the raft they were dismantling. David set to work with a will and ignored the other two, who were making a couple of crude paddles: if Michael were with him, nothing could go wrong. Over his head the boys were discussing him.

"I can't get used to the idea that we can talk about him while he's here," said Peter. "It seems all wrong."

"Why doesn't he wear a hearing aid?" asked Dick.

"Because it wouldn't be any use to him," said Michael. "He's too deaf. He's never heard a single human voice."

"Never at all?"

"No. At least, Eric says that they have an instrument at the school which amplifies sound loud enough for David to hear something. He loves it. But what he hears is very little."

As David continued working contentedly, the others sat back on their heels while Michael told them something of what he had learnt from Eric and from David himself. Presently David looked up, saw them talking to Michael, and wondered why they were not doing any work. Michael was his friend, the others were not, and he did not want to share Michael with them. Peter saw his glance and remarked:

"I can't stand the way he looks at me. It gives me the creeps."

"Why?" asked Michael.

"I don't know. It just does."

"But he's got to look. It's the only way he has of knowing anything."

"I've nothing against people like him, but I just don't want to have anything to do with them."

"Would you keep out of the way of someone who's blind?"

"Of course not. That's different."

"Why?"

"Well, it's terrible to be blind."

"It's terrible to be totally deaf."

"But it's not the same."

"Why?"

"Well, they're dumb, stupid, simple. They're not normal, almost loony, and I don't like loonies."

"But can't you see," burst out Michael, "that's just where you're wrong? Oh, I know David sometimes looks a dimwit—and acts like one; but if he could hear, he'd be just like us. He could talk, and read, and learn, and—oh, everything!"

Peter, however, was not to be convinced and came back to his first point, adding:

"I still think you're a bit soft about his being deaf."

All this time David had been energetically heaving out nails, but now he wanted a rest. He tugged at Michael's arm and passed him the pincers. He made a gesture as though to mop his brow, to indicate he was hot and tired. Michael got up to continue the work, and, rather than be left sitting next to David, Peter joined him.

Dick was left with David, who smiled at him briefly. He smiled back, thinking that the poor kid looked scared (for he was at least a couple of years older than David). David said something aloud that he could not recognize as any word or words. He shook his head, and knitting his fingers together pointed first to David and then to himself. David understood, and began patiently to teach him the finger-alphabet, until they were interrupted by the arrival of some other boys with more planks.

In the general hustle that followed David sat aside to watch. After much deliberating and measurement the boys set to work again, and Michael came to sit beside him.

"We make two boats," he wrote, and drew a diagram of how the rafts were to be built.

The work went ahead. There were not enough tools to go round, but the next day, Friday, David was given the privilege of knocking the nails into the last plank. Then a line was drawn along each edge of the rafts, so that the planks could be sawn an even length to make paddling easier. While this was being done Michael spelled for David:

"Finished."

David looked puzzled and shook his head.

"Yes, nearly finished," Michael repeated.

David pointed to the rafts, put up his little finger, which is the equivalent of "thumbs down"—"no good"—and shook his head again.

"What?" asked Michael.

David repeated his gesture, and said aloud: "Bad. No good."

"Why?" asked Michael. Hearing David speak the other boys had looked up.

"He says the rafts are no good," Michael explained with a tolerant smile.

"And whatever does he know about it?" asked one boy.

"He's trying to be clever again," said Peter.

"Wait a bit and I'll find out what he's on about," said Michael. His friends had grudgingly agreed to David's joining them: they had done so largely to please Michael and because they secretly admired the fact that David had walked through the tunnel, a feat that they had often considered but never carried out. Now Michael realized that he was going to have more difficulty than he had thought in persuading them to accept David. Reaching for the paper and pencil he wrote:

"What is wrong?"

David shrugged his shoulders. He did not know exactly what was wrong with the boats, but he knew they were no good. All his holidays had been spent on the seashore, and he had used his eyes and had unconsciously absorbed the shape, and balance of things made to float. He had not questioned that Michael and his friends, with all the advantages of their hearing, did not know what he knew. But these were town boys, and many of them had not had even a canal to play on before they moved to the housing estate.

"Balance" was a word David did not know, but he could act it. Standing in the middle of one of the rafts and over its central keel, he stretched his arms out level and steady on each side, then he leaned out to the side as though to ply a paddle, but could not reach the water. He demonstrated that, in order to paddle, the crew would have to sit off-center, and that the whole raft would then overbalance.

They shook their heads and laughed at him, not unkindly, for his performance was both expressive and explicit.

"Wood floats," wrote Michael; but David did not understand. He changed it to "wood stays up in water," and then to "wood swims," before David nodded his head impatiently.

"Of course," he signed, but he repeated aloud: "Boa' no good. Boa' no good." He would have started his demonstration all over again, but they laughingly dissuaded him, and carried on with their trimming and the fashioning of the paddles.

"He's a terrific actor," said Dick.

"Yes," agreed Michael. "It's amazing what he can explain by miming."

"But he does get some odd ideas."

"Yes. Why on earth should he think the rafts were no good?"

"Perhaps he doesn't like the water."

"Could be. And I still don't know what he meant by seeing faces in the tunnel!"

"In spite of everything, he's still a bit odd."

As they talked about him, David sat aside and glowered. He knew he was right, and was annoyed that they would not listen. Even Michael had laughed at him.

He conjured up a mental picture of the launching: Michael would step on the raft off-center and would slide into the water as the whole thing rolled over. David himself would laugh at him from the towpath. The picture pleased him, and he embellished it with a sequel: himself helping Michael out of the water, and then the boys asking him to show them what was wrong with the boats. As he watched them now, he smiled to himself in a way that almost said: "I told you so."

Nevertheless, that evening he took his problem to Eric, and in his own way told him why the boats were no good. Eric promised to have a look at them tomorrow afternoon, Saturday, when he had come back from work.

12

∗ *A ducking*

There was a crowd of boys and girls along the towpath when Eric strolled good-humoredly down to see if David's fears were correct and what was happening. Paul and Tommy were there, getting in everyone's way and begging to be the first on board after the launching; and Eileen was with a couple of her friends watching from the fringe. As Eric joined them, Michael and Dick heaved up one of the rafts, swung it between them, and dropped it into the canal. It caught the brick wall edging the water, slid in crookedly, water sloshing across the boards, and finally settled on an even keel to the dying motion of the waves it had created.

"Watch us!" cried one of the other boys. "We'll make a better launching than that. Come on."

"Wait a minute," said Eric, stepping forward. "You're not going to use those things as rafts, are you?"

"Yes, of course."

"Why not? They float."

"Oh, yes, they float, but they'll turn turtle as soon as you put any weight near the edge. Look, give me a paddle. Thanks. Now anyone with a grain of sense would know that as soon as you push it one side goes right under. See?"

The boys voiced their disappointment as they watched Eric's demonstration wash away their afternoon's sport.

"A Boy Scout wouldn't put a thing like this on a rain puddle," he continued.

"But what can we do about it?" Peter asked.

"You'll have to make them more substantial. They'll need at least another sleeper down each side. One in the middle doesn't give any support at the sides, and the raft is too wide for someone to sit dead center and paddle."

"Coo! We thought we'd get four of us on each of them."

"Would have been a wet outing," was Eric's brief comment. "Can you get any more sleepers from anywhere?"

"Oh, we should be able to find some."

"Is that what David was trying to tell us yesterday?" asked Michael.

"Yes, that's right. You know he's not nearly so dim as you might think—at least not about anything he does know."

Michael gave David a wink of acknowledgement, and David beamed all over his face.

"I know where there are some old sleepers," burst out Tommy. "Down by the old tip."

As they discussed ways and means of improving their craft, Ted was walking up toward them from the village. He had decided to come back along the towpath, where he knew there would be the usual crowd of children, but he was not expecting to find older boys there, too. When he saw David and Eric he nearly turned back. The boys all seemed too much engrossed in whatever it was they were doing to notice him, or he might at least have made a detour. As it was, he thought that he could probably pass them without being seen. He would have done so had he not been tempted to give Eric's ankle a kick in passing. Eric yelped and cried out:

"Hey, look out! That hurt. Oh, it's you, is it?" and he stood up. "Was it you who kicked me?"

"If you stick your feet out on the path you've got to expect a kick or two."

"Haven't you already done enough damage without barging around kicking on purpose?"

"Who's talking about damage?"

The boys gathered behind Eric, leaving the ground clear for the two older boys. Only David stood apart.

"I don't know how you've got the nerve to show your squashed sprout of a face round here after the way you treated my brother."

"I haven't touched your little brother."

"Oh, no, you didn't egg them on to hunt him down, did you?"

"And what was he doing but being a beastly little show-off?"

"Come on and fight, or are you too much of a coward even for that?"

Ted hit out first, but Eric was prepared and sidestepped. Then he attacked with both fists, catching Ted on the shoulder. The boys gathered round to cheer Eric on. David only knew that his brother was hitting Ted, and hitting hard.

Ted had the advantage of a heavier build, but he had lost his temper and was blustering, whereas Eric was determined to beat once and for all this boy who had taken such a mean advantage of David. He was certainly scoring the greater number of hits, and might have knocked Ted down, had not he himself tripped and fallen over the raft that was still beside the path. Ted was on him before he had time to get to his feet, and began to pummel his head. Eric grabbed his wrists and started to kick. What had begun as a clean but hot-blooded fight broke into an all-out wrestling match, each of the opponents trying to roll the other into the canal. For a while they rolled back and forth on the towpath, neither gaining over the other, until for want of breath they paused and scrambled to their feet. Eric had a bleeding hand, which he had grazed on a stone, and a cut on his chin. Ted was limping badly. Gasping and panting but otherwise silent, they faced each other warily again.

"Go on, Eric," shouted someone. "Lam him a good one!"

"Chuck him in the water!"

Eric sprang and caught Ted squarely on the chin. Ted tried to steady himself on his injured leg, but his knee gave way, and he stepped on to the raft that was on the water. It began to tip over with his weight. In an effort to save himself from going right under, he grabbed at the far edge of the raft, now standing nearly upright in the water. He only succeeded in pulling it over his head.

For a few minutes Ted was entirely submerged beneath the upturned raft, and only one of his hands was visible, vainly gripping its edge.

During the short silence that followed, David, though he could not have expressed it in words signed, written, or spoken, saw himself vindicated on two counts. Ted's bullying at the time of the football game was now wiped out by Eric's victory; and his own description of the "Boa' no good" was proved accurate. The easiest way to express his satisfaction was to laugh, and he let rip with great guffaws. The other boys were almost as pleased, though more restrained.

Ted freed himself and floundered to the bank to face a row of grinning faces. He climbed out, and limped homewards, followed by jeers.

David nudged Michael for attention, stuck up both his

thumbs, and grinned broadly. Michael responded with a wink.

Eric sighed with satisfaction. "I've been wanting to have that fight for a long while."

"It was time someone sat on him good and proper. Perhaps he'll be a bit more bearable now," said Michael.

13

* *The swans' nest*

It rained that Sunday, so nothing further was done to improve the rafts until several evenings later. Tommy, with Paul, had found a pile of old sleepers on a rubbish dump near the railway yard, and one evening the boys staggered up to the canal carrying some half-dozen of the best looking. Now that they had seen the weakness of their first attempt, they were determined to make the rafts worthy of the heaviest weather they were likely to encounter on the canal.

They built two square frames, which was what they should have done in the beginning, lashing the sleepers together in the best shipshape fashion, before nailing the planks across the whole. They worked during the evenings while the light lasted and over a couple of weekends. It was towards the end of September before they had the rafts ready for launching again, but this time they were heaved on to the water with both Eric's and David's approval.

Tommy and Paul were given the privilege of being first on

board; and, because they jumped on too eagerly, the raft rocked and Tommy nearly lost his balance. When some of the others stepped on more cautiously, it settled evenly on the water. Presently two noisy parties of the older boys, including David, were paddling happily along the canal.

It was the last, still, warm day of summer, a golden time to spend on the water. At first they had some difficulty in learning to control their craft, to paddle them forward rather than in circles. Soon they found the knack of paddling in time. They began to race each other from the footbridge to the corner where the canal divided, one branch leading to the tunnel, the other into Bitter End.

The boys were learning to accept David, though they relied on Michael to communicate with him when necessary. David had been willing to do the less interesting jobs of raft-building largely because explanation of anything else became so complicated. He was usually cheerful and could always be relied on to enjoy thoroughly the slapstick horseplay that accompanied their work. He often rolled around in fits of laughter that would set everyone else off. They had often pretended to hit a finger with the hammer for the pleasure of watching his broad grin dissolve into bellowing laughter.

But it was to Michael that David always turned for information or approval. Michael had become not only his first hearing friend, which was an achievement in itself, but also for the time being his only attachment outside his own family. David had just started the term at his new school. It had come as something of a shock to find that he had to begin to make new friends, to learn the ways of new teachers, new classrooms and corridors, and new rules. Coming home every evening to his family, and Michael's continuing friendship, helped him.

Now, on this weekend holiday, he was sitting cross-legged on the boat behind Michael and helping to paddle the cumbersome craft. Michael's instructions and his own sense of the water were sufficient to make him at least as good a member of the crew as any of the others. Dick and Peter sitting on his right were surprised and thankful that he was not proving an embarrassment or a handicap. He entered into the spirit of the races as fiercely as anyone else, and, when they stopped racing for want of breath, shared the pleasure of drifting silently on the water.

Bitter End and the outer reaches of the town were set slightly below the canal level, so that the roar of traffic and machinery was reduced to a gentle hum. The brick edging of the towpath, with its far wall on one side and the reeds and growth along the bank by the hillside, enclosed them in a narrow belt of water and greenery. To this was added the fascination of familiar surroundings seen from a new angle: the level of the water below the towpath made the reeds appear taller, wilder, and more luscious; the brick wall became a quay large enough for a steamer to dock at; and Windbell Edge disappeared behind its own height and curves, to bulk the size of a mountain.

To the illusion of this mixture of country and dockland was added mystery, magic, and power, as a pair of swans flew almost directly towards them from out of the sunlight. On the soft southwesterly breeze the beating rhythm of the wings could be heard with its accompanying whine, not quite a musical note, nor so crude as the whine of a jet engine, but demanding the whole of one's attention down to the fingertips gripping the paddle.

"There they are," whispered Dick, pointing above the sun. The two swans were silhouetted as dark shadows, dark against the sky, but were in themselves a luminous gray that shone like silver at the edge of the wings, where the sunlight penetrated the fineness of the feathers.

David was watching the ripples around the paddle with which he was caressing the water, when Michael nudged him. He was in time to watch the two birds rise with the wind that lifted them up the hillside, their necks stretched out in that faintly ridiculous shape not unlike a spoon handle, and which bore little resemblance to their curves when on the water. As the angle of vision altered in relation to the sunlight the gray silhouettes changed to the shining whiteness of clouds, punctuated at either end by the sharp darkness of the feet and beaks. The musical beat of the wings was cut suddenly as the birds flew out of sight above the hill.

"They must have come from the reservoir."

"They might have landed here," said Michael, "if we hadn't been on the water."

"Let's go and find the old swans' nest around the bend," suggested Peter. "I've never seen it close up."

The other raft had drifted off towards the lock gates in Bitter End, so they followed their own course. They went up the branch of the canal that led to the tunnel, and to the small almost overgrown basin that had been dug out of the hillside for some long forgotten purpose. Here, among the reeds which crowded out the water, protected by the cliff and undisturbed by the canal traffic, a pair of swans nested each year. They could be glimpsed occasionally from the towpath on the other side of the water, a gleam of white feathers, sitting patiently among the green and brown reeds; or the top of the head and eyes stretched and peering over the stalks.

The boys crashed their raft through the narrow entrance, using the paddles like punting poles to push against the mass of reeds and mud. Having broken through the barrier, they found themselves in a narrow strip of water covered with duckweed and barely wider than the raft itself. At one end was a brown shapeless pillar that might have been the decayed stump of a tree. When they examined this more closely, it proved to have been built of mud, reeds, and droppings. Only a few bedraggled feathers clinging miserably to the mud and droppings, showed that this was a nest. Michael tried to explain to David:

"S-W-A-N-S-N-E-S-T," he spelled on his fingers.

David did not seem to understand.

"S-W-A-N-B-I-G-W-H-I-T-E-B-I-R-D," spelled Michael.

David nodded, and with his fingers and wrist made a fluid movement that exactly expressed the head and curves of a swan's neck, and ended as the fold of the wings over its back. Yes, he knew what a swan was, but (pointing at the messy stump) this was not a nest. He cupped his hands in the cozy shape of all nests he had ever seen or handled.

"Ness'," he said, "ness'."

Michael smiled and nodded. He understood David's difficulty, but could do no more than repeat his information. David refused to accept it, and the boys all laughed with him when, with that gesture which expresses a bad smell, he held his nose with one hand, put up the little finger of the other, for "thumbs down," and turned his back on the shapeless muck heap. A beautiful and great bird like the swan had no right to make and use such a miserable thing.

They pushed the raft away and settled down to enjoy the unexpected seclusion of the backwater. Because there was not space for them to lie down, they eased their cramped positions by sitting back to back, and lapsed into silence. Even the canal wall was hidden now by banks of reeds which shivered at the slightest breath of air and shimmered in the afternoon sun that warmed the hollow. The bulrush heads were swelling under their dark brown velvet cases. The mass of duckweed covering the water resembled the magnified cells of some living organism as seen through a microscope, shifting, heaving, actively

alive as a single unit, but in reality a hundred thousand sepa-
rate particles.

The lower slopes of Windbell Edge, or what could be seen
of them, looked a different shape, and might have led up to
mountain tops and crags more dramatic and wild than the hill
they knew.

The little tinkles, plops, scratches, sighs, rustles, and drips
became loud and important. It was difficult to remember they
were always happening: they had been happening last year,
yesterday, this afternoon while the rafts were racing and before the secluded basin had been found; they would still be
tinkling, plopping, and sighing through the night and all next
week, whether anyone was there to hear them or not. The
lapping between the wooden sleepers of the raft and the
boards on which they were sitting became almost inaudible as
the water settled to its usual stagnant calm. If one of the boys
shifted his weight the flip-flop of the wavelets could be heard
running the length of the raft. Having left its cover, they
could be seen undulating with the duckweed, to be lost among
the faintest rasping of the sharp edges of the reeds.

A sudden plop of water immediately beneath them was so
loud in comparison that they almost heard the raft protest.

"A fish," said Dick.

"A tiddler, more likely," said Peter.

"That is a fish."

"Not what I call a fish."

They were too bemused to bother to look for it, and anyway
it would have gone by now. Michael drew up his knees, folded
his arms around them, and with pleasure smelled the warm
tangy scent of the sun on his arm. From somewhere high
above and over the hill they could hear at intervals the notes of
a lark that spilled softly into their hidden basin. A train whistle was the only noise of the town that reached them, and even

that had an illusion of remoteness and mystery, to set the imagination off on new travels.

Presently Peter spoke:

"You know," he said, "I see what you mean now about the deaf. How did he know our first rafts were no good? Who could teach him that, and how can he learn anything except what he can see?"

"I don't know about the rafts," Michael replied. "It's a mystery to me, too."

"I can't imagine what it's like not to hear a single thing. Nothing, nothing at all," Peter continued. "If you close your eyes you can't see anything and you can get an idea of what it's like to be blind. But you can't stop hearing things—even if you try to."

This was an unusually long and profound speech for Peter to have made, and no one knew what to say next. Having started thinking aloud, he went on:

"Fancy never having heard a jazz band, or a pop singer, or snare drums, or the crowds cheering at a soccer match, or a four-engine turbo-jet air liner, or—or——"

"—a 500 cc roaring down the straight—the bang of a six-shooter in a western."

"And the little things," added Michael.

"Yes, but those are easier to imagine because you don't hear them as a rule—like that lark singing. We wouldn't have heard it if we'd been talking."

"What about talking itself? That's not loud. Suppose you couldn't hear your own voice."

"That beats me. I can't imagine it. I just can't."

"And your own footsteps," Michael continued, "and money in your pocket, brushing your teeth, and your tummy rumbling, and—the crunch of biting an apple."

"Yes, I know. But if it's really quiet you sort of feel cut off, even if there are little sounds. I like plenty of noise all the time—it's friendly like. If you can hear the radio, and the traffic and trains you know you're not alone."

All this time David was sitting with his back propped against Michael's. He had taken off his sandals and had been dipping his feet in the water, where the little-green-water-leaves (for he knew no other name for duckweed) had tangled with his toes and now clung limply. Having picked them off his feet, he began wiggling his toes to dry them, and at the same time he was amusing himself by tearing apart a blade of reed. By running his fingernail in the right direction he found that the leaf split cleanly down its length, and he was splitting each half into smaller, narrower lengths, narrower and thinner, until finally he had one as thin as a sewing-string, and his fingers had become stained a greenish brown. He threw the remnants of the reed away, and allowed his eyes to wander over the immediate scene.

He knew the other two boys were losing their fear of him, or rather he knew by their relaxed attitudes that they were no longer suspicious and hostile. They were not watching him any longer, either with a full-faced stare or surreptitiously from the corners of their eyes.

He leaned back to feel the sun on his face and Michael's bony spine fitting in alongside his own. Michael's rate of breathing did not correspond with his. At one point they would breathe in together, but, as David's pace was faster, there was a series of overlapping and rippling muscular movements, like two people walking side by side whose footsteps crisscross. Then David would breathe out and Michael in at the same moment. The whole sequence was repeated, or it might have been repeated if Michael had not spoken.

David knew it immediately, partly by the disturbance of Michael's breathing, and partly by the tingling that came from somewhere beneath Michael's shoulder blades, weaker than he might have felt with his fingers on Michael's cheeks or throat, but unmistakable for all that. He stopped breathing and tensed himself slightly, so as not to lose the sensation that was always pleasurable, whether it came from people or from things, such as the radio, the bodywork of a moving car, or the windowpane when heavy traffic was passing. He was "listening" to Michael through his body, and it gave him a greater sense of companionship and knowledge of what was happening. The vibrations were so weak that he was not sure that Michael had stopped speaking until his breathing became normal. He glanced up at Dick sitting by his side, and with his back against Peter's. Yes, Dick was talking now, and looked surprised when he saw David watching him. (Privately Dick agreed with Peter. David was uncanny at times. He had looked up the moment he had started to speak, exactly as though he were listening; but Dick made no comment.)

David settled himself comfortably again, pressing his back against Michael's. He did not want to miss the effect of Michael's speaking, that came to him spasmodically, broad and gentle as the beat of a butterfly's wings, delicate as the six legs of a ladybird walking across the palm of his hand, and at the same time both warm and friendly. He watched the little-green-water-leaves rising and falling as a body to the slight motion of the raft, and the wavelets spreading into the reeds, and would have been content to stay until sunset.

Presently Peter stirred and shifted his position. David knew it was Peter even though he could not see him, and that seemed to be the signal for them to leave. David picked up his paddle and helped to push and drag the raft back through the reeds into the canal. They paddled along slowly now, savoring the last hour of the shortening afternoon. Tommy and Paul had found them and trotted beside them along the towpath, their mouths opening and shutting continuously; but David made no attempt to lip-read, for he still had to watch Michael's paddling movements carefully.

It had been a good day altogether. Boat good; Michael good; Dick good; Peter? Yes, Peter good. Swan good. Swans' nest? No, swans' nest bad. And he smiled as he remembered it. Racing good; black dirty water good. Black. Black?

David looked up from Michael's paddle and the drops falling from it into the water, to see that they were approaching the tunnel. To his dismay he realized the boys were going to enter.

14

* *The tunnel again*

The pace of their paddling had quickened and they were leaning forward as though to hasten the approach of darkness. David stopped paddling and tapped Michael's shoulder.

"No, no, off," he said aloud. They smiled at him, beckoned to him, pointed to the tunnel, and tried to persuade him.

"No. Off, off."

At last they pushed the raft to the side, where David surrendered his place and his paddle to Tommy, who jumped nimbly aboard almost before David had gained the security of the path. Paul was also allowed on to the raft.

David set off home, happy and satisfied. He did not ask much of life, and so he treasured all the more the few golden moments that had been his during the afternoon. He knew he had gained something positive without the need of language. It was good and he accepted it gladly.

"You'd think he was scared," Tommy remarked as he sat in

David's place and picked up the paddle still warm and slightly damp from his grip. "Was he?"

"Why should he be?" Dick countered. "You stop talking and watch what you're doing."

They subsided into silence as the raft was paddled slowly, to allow for Tommy's age, into the tunnel. They felt almost as though they were being drawn in slow motion down a giant drainpipe.

They had frequently ventured along the towpath for the sake of defying authority as well as out of curiosity, but being on the water in itself added a glamour the tunnel had never had before. They planned to go farther in than usual.

"Supposing we meet a barge coming towards us. What happens then?" asked Paul, his voice already echoing.

"We'd see it against the light at the other end, and we'd hear the motor," said Michael.

"It would run us down and then we'd be shipwrecked."

"'Shipwrecked in a tunnel—it sounds mad."

"In the middle of a hill in the middle of England."

"With the nearest lifeboat a hundred miles away."

"They'd have to bring it by helicopter, and launch it at Blackley to come to our rescue."

"And slide it down the factory roof into the water."

"Why?" asked Tommy.

"All good lifeboats are launched down a slide."

"Like the one at the baths only bigger?"

"Yes. We could even borrow that one for the occasion."

Talking nonsense—nonsense reverberating down the length of dark brick walls and black water. A raft made of railway sleepers floating down a tunnel built a couple of hundred years ago. Obsolete, out-of-date nonsense. Michael smiled to himself as he paddled into the blacker darkness.

Meanwhile, Tommy would not admit that he was becoming

tired, that it was hard and heavy work paddling, and that he was rubbing a blister on his hand.

As they moved slowly forward, their eyes became accustomed to the darkness and they were able to steer a sufficiently straight course, though now and again they found the raft drifting to one side or the other, and they bumped it off the wall or towpath. After a while Michael noticed they were hitting the left hand wall more frequently, the side on which he and Tommy were sitting, and he paddled more strongly to counteract the drift. When his paddle scraped along the wall again, he said:

"Tommy, you're not paddling."

"I am."

"D'you want a rest?"

"Yes."

Peter brought a box of matches from his pocket, and the sudden explosive flare took them by surprise—not because it was unexpected but because the brightness of the small flame was a much greater contrast than seemed possible, drawing their eyes to the light even as they blinked against the hurt. It was so bright that they could see nothing beyond their own ghostly faces in a ring round it. The flame lasted a few seconds before Peter dropped it on the water to snap out with a sizzle. Then the blackness hit their eyes as hard as the light had done.

It was a small thing that changed the whole atmosphere from one of adventurous expectancy to unease and misgiving. As they sat still to allow the whirling black shapes and dazzling nothings on their eyeballs to settle and fade, the raft was drifting to the end of its last paddled momentum. Tommy was holding the edge with one hand partly to rest his tired arm, partly to make sure he knew where the edge was. His cry when his knuckles were scraped and imprisoned against the rough brick wall made the other four jump. They jerked the raft sharply and provoked another even louder cry that in the confined darkness echoed horribly.

"What's the matter?"

"Strike another match."

"Tommy, what is it?"

"My hand—oh! my hand. Push the raft off."

"Where are you?"

"Which way?"

Peter struck another match as Tommy freed his hand and held it to the light.

"It's only a graze. It's not that bad."

"Cor! You made enough noise to blow the roof off."

"Wrap your hanky round it."

"Haven't got one," and Tommy whimpered as the match went out and the blackness again smothered them.

"Here," said Michael, "take my hanky and lick the blood off before you wrap it round. Got it?"

"I think there's only one match left," said Peter. "Shall I strike it?"

"No, better keep it."

"Oh, my hand hurts! My hand hurts!"

"Of course it hurts," Michael reassured him. "You can't expect to come out on an adventure and not get hurt, can you?"

"I want to go home."

"But we've hardly gone any way yet," said Dick. "I've walked farther than this along the path."

"Change with Paul, Tommy. He can paddle now," said Michael.

"I want to go home," Tommy repeated in a voice that was near tears.

"Well, get off and walk back while we go on."

"No."

"Then you'll have to sit tight and come with us. Careful, Paul! Don't rock us so much."

"Here, Tommy," said Dick. "Have a sweet. It's a bit old but it's all right."

"I don't want it. I want to go home."

"We will soon, but we're going a bit farther first."

"We've only come about a hundred yards," said Dick.

"Oh, it's more than that," Peter protested. "At least a quarter of a mile."

"It can't be. The other end doesn't look any closer. Come on."

They started paddling again, determined not to give in so easily. They remained quiet now, and only a few sniffs from Tommy, the splash of water, and an occasional scrape of a paddle on brick broke the silence.

Michael set his eyes on the distant light as though it were a guiding beacon, the only thing to be seen, though it was more than a mile away, a small round hole in the blackness like a miniature moon. As he watched, it began to move. He blinked his eyes to correct the illusion but that had the opposite effect, for the light realistically blinked back at him, a huge single shining eye in a face of blackness. He glanced over his shoulder to the nearer entrance to relieve his eyes, and was met by a gray-white circle that stared at him blankly, expressionless, a face without features. He looked forward again into the darkness, and out of it jumped the shining eye, dancing in time to his quickening pulse.

"So that's what it was," he said aloud.

"What?" asked Dick.

"He kept on talking about faces—faces in the tunnel, and we couldn't make out what he meant."

"Oh, have you been seeing them too?" asked Peter. "I thought it was only me."

"Yes, so've I," Dick acknowledged. "They've been giving me the creeps for the last ten minutes. And he walked all the way through—another whole mile of it!"

"He must have nerves of iron," Peter said in a tone that implied he himself would prefer to keep his own weaker nerves and be spared the ordeal.

"Yes," agreed Michael. "Or perhaps he was more frightened of everything else."

"How do you mean?"

"Of people—people not understanding him, people hunting him as if he were a fox or a hare."

"Mike!" cried Tommy through suppressed tears. "I want to go home."

"Yes. We're going right now."

They left the tunnel to its own secret isolation and eeriness, and returned to the security of the warmth and light of home and to hot sizzling suppers. Each of them found that his tentative liking of David had grown to admiration. Along with his deafness, he became known henceforth as the boy who had been all the way through the tunnel. He had achieved something which no one else had yet had the courage to complete.